It was a Rogue, its hands encasing Thomas' skull . . . There was no resistance . . . The Rogue saw him. Stood over Thomas' body like an animal protecting its kill. Its face had no lines to give it age, was only smeared with a mixture of blood and dirt not its own. The torso and legs were gouged. Its mouth opened, and the sounds that rumbled toward him were less words than snarls. Parric took a step back, and the Rogue lifted its arms like battering rams and charged.

also by Charles L. Grant

THE SHADOW OF ALPHA

ASCENSION

CHARLES L. GRANT

A BERKLEY MEDALLION BOOK
published by
BERKLEY PUBLISHING CORPORATION

For Ian.

**Whose name, whatever the translation,
is synonomous with joy.**

I

SUNSET IN THE mountains of the east: trees billowing to behemouth shadows, lakes calming under a darkening sky. Dusk to starlight, and a nightwind rises to scatter pockets of the afternoon's heat. A colony of bats surfaces like black smoke, wheels and scatters; a colony of insects sweeps out of a valley, noiselessly, invisibly. There is a moon before midnight, and a grey sheen that bleaches the ground in irregular patches, a shooting star that dies before the horizon, and constellations that prowl behind the seasons.

A road. Huddled against wooded slopes, diving swiftly into shadowpools and climbing to stretch for air. Deserted. Retreating. Five decades of winter gouging churning its surface into rutted, pitted desolation.

Within a ragged circle of darkened stones a fire sparked down to embers. It flared once and briefly when a leaf settled onto the coals, then became sullen again until Parric goaded it with another awkward tier of twigs that took several careful puffs of breath and wind before popping into blue-gold flame. He blinked against the sudden glare, then settled back against the rotted stump of a crippled pine. The bark grated through his dusty cloak, the cleared earth around the fire was coldly damp, but comfort was a luxury that would have to wait its turn.

He shivered, and grunted.

He tossed a chip into the flames and jumped when it snapped and spat into the air.

"Brave," he muttered to himself, and pulled the cloak closer to this throat. His stomach growled, but dawn was the time for eating—a discipline he hated for its necessity. He dozed, then, and flame-flickering images of his traveling became a pulsing sequence of dreams so monotonously familiar that his sleep quickly deepened, and his head lowered slowly until it rested on his upraised knees.

You'll come, of course.

No, Father, I don't think I will.

Well, don't you think you've reached an age when something ought to be done? Not that I want you to think I'm pressing, Orion.

Each man has his task, is that it, Father? Each man has to do his part for the betterment of mankind?

Betterment at this stage has nothing to do with it. What we need now are points for survival.

That sounds like you're quoting Grandfather again. Tell me something—did he have a saying for everything?

It wasn't a saying, damnit, it was sense! We can't afford to insulate ourselves the way others have. We have to consolidate and confederate. Reach out and consolidate again. It's the only way, and you know it even if you don't want to admit it. Let's face it, son, we've come a long way in such a short time.

A long way toward what? Toward rebuilding? To what end, Father? To what end are you and all the rest of them trying to kill us before our time? So we can stumble like idiots into another accidental war and send out another Plague? Why bother? It's going to happen, you know. It's the nature of the species.

A rock split and Parric snapped his head, his arms instantly freeing themselves from the confines of the cloak. There was a dagger in his left hand, another in his right, and he scanned the dawn shadows anxiously until he spotted the source of his awakening. And even at that, the tension in his limbs refused to subside until he'd risen to his feet and had made a cautious search of the area around his campsite, and a careful testing of the wind.

When he was satisfied, he allowed himself a morning smile.

A bird exploded out of the tree above him, and he strained to follow its flight, grinning when he saw two others rise to join it. The crowherds, he thought, would have a field day working these woods. It would be easy enough, far easier than back home, to trap the nesting pairs and transport them to places where they were needed to protect the crops. Insects were still overabundant, but here the balance seemed to be returning to normal—or what he supposed normal had been before the Plague Wind had swept across most of the planet and left the dregs to the serpents and spiders. It was a difficult job, being a crowherd, working in teams to lure back the birds; but they, at least, seemed to be accomplishing something tangible, and lasting.

Even his brother Mathew had gotten into the salvation act, but Parric considered his work the most futile: prowling the mountains, rooting out enclaves of humanity to convince them the ContiGov had in fact survived reasonably intact—and needed them to reestablish civilization before it tottered further and collapsed into savage rubble. Idealistic benevolence. It smacked of dreaming, and Parric refused to sanction it. Regrettably, Mathew had become too much like the rest of the family—imbued with Grandfather's visions of reunification.

And why?

"For history, why not?" the old man had said. As though that had bestowed upon the struggle a messianic blessing.

3

"For goddamned history!" Parric spat at the ground, and busied himself with what would pass for his breakfast. Nutrient tablets and a palmful of paste to give him the illusion of being sated. A handful of cold water from a nearby stream to clear out his eyes, waken his face, wash the tasteless pap from his mouth. Then he squatted on the grassy bank and watched his face reform continuously in the flowing clear water: large, like the rest of him, dark-skinned with eyes green enough to be mistaken for black. A heavy thatch of long brown hair and beard, split down the right side by a vivid blond streak, the sole physical legacy of his mother's sufferings to bear him. He tugged thoughtfully at the tangle on his chin, scratched bits of leaves and grass from his neck and head. Then rubbed a finger alongside his nose in prelude to a morning ritual.

He could always go back. It was as simple as that. Go back to Town Central and the machines he monitored and the androids he tested and the frantic grasping of less than three hundred people to keep alive the knowledge and skills of unnumbered centuries.

He could always go back.

Like hell.

A rustling, and he whirled with one hand darting toward the top of his boot. A red squirrel raced through the underbrush, its puffed tail raised in alarm.

Cocky little bastard, he thought as he returned to camp. But he was smiling when the squirrel and its young ones followed to gambol in the high branches. He waved at them, laughed when they scolded, then fussed with his backpack until it rested on his shoulders with a minimum of stress.

He stretched. Felt the air. Turned on his heels until he was nearly dizzy.

It would be too warm again to wear the cloak. That pleased him. But it would also be warm enough to tire him easily and cut down the distance of his traveling. That made him impatient before he started out.

A final check and the burying of the fire, and he stared down the gentle ten-meter slope to the road. Beyond was a drop to a second road, beyond that a shallow valley not yet shed of its nightfall. Peaceful, certainly, though he refused to move until the voices of the mountains had reassured him of their safety. He had learned quickly not to depend on his eyesight alone. Too often he'd stumbled upon Hunters' spoors freshly made, and freshly dangerous. They wouldn't have come from Central. He was too far East for that. And Hunters who wouldn't recognize him for the innocent he was would down him first, without compunction.

And a month onto the road he'd come across the rotted remains of a small family group viciously murdered: quartered, with their limbs strewn obscenely over the landscape. He hadn't doubted from the first that they'd been victims of a Rogue attack, and he'd been frightened into a day's immobility. The experts at Central had led him to believe that all the Rogues had either been finally destroyed or rendered relatively harmless by time's loss of power.

Obviously a mistake, and there were still nights when he thought and tried not to think of the Plague-damaged androids and the mindlessness with which they slaughtered anything that moved.

So he listened. For an hour while the sun rose whitely, bleaching the sharp morning blue from the sky ahead of it. But there was nothing but birdsong, insects, and the faint splattering from the stream behind him.

"Go," he told his shadow, and he scrambled down the bank and struck out along the roadbed. Heading eastward. Searching the road, the ditches, the overhanging branches of heavily leaved trees for signs of his father's passing.

5

Three years before, Dorin Parric and eight other fools had traveled this same route. One way.

Willard will be coming with me, Orion.

Good for him. It'll be like old times, then, won't it? First he takes Grandfather on the road to Philayork, and brings back his body. Now he'll be following you. Aren't you a little nervous?

I don't intend to die on the way, Orion. I'm going to look around, that's all. Willard will be useful if we come across a village or town. We can show him as an example that all androids aren't dangerous, that we've engineered out the breakdowns. We can teach them that all the Willards we have now are vital to their survival.

Sure.

I don't understand you, Orion. I wish to hell I did.

It's not just me, Father.

I know. That's why I have to go. And you will take care of your mother for me. But please, listen to me just this once. Don't worry her by getting into those damned nihilistic arguments. She, at least, understands what I have to do.

Good. That makes one of us.

Two years ago. A bitterly cold inhuman February twilight. Willard, battered and near to dying, had returned to Town Central with Dorin's body wrapped in a midnight green cloak. The tiny expedition had indeed reached Philayork, and something else. A kingdom ruled by a petty and bloated self-proclaimed tyrant. A ragged band, according to Willard, who'd been waiting for them and stubbornly refused Dorin's attempts at conference and negotiation. They'd attacked instead. Killed all but Dorin who survived his wounds long enough to see the mountains again. Willard had returned him to be interred beside

6

the body of his wife. She had been murdered by a Rogue that had penetrated the Town's weak defenses not two months after her husband had left to die in a graveyard.

The voices spurred, the memories nagged, and by noon Parric spotted the first signs of Philayork's approach. The road widened, no less battered, and every few kilometers were charred ruins of housing clusters, destroyed by the remnants of a panicked population fleeing the city in unreasonable hope that the Plague wasn't airborne, wasn't as widespread as their viones claimed before the bulletins were castrated by their own hysteria.

But it had been, and it was.

Another ContiGov milestone, Parric thought bitterly. When the Plague broke out in the midst of a Eurccom war, the means of immunization had been shipped secretly to the Noram continent and just as secretly were its citizens inoculated. There was, however, neither enough serum nor enough time to synthesize. When the Plague finally arrived—whether by accident or design being a fatally moot point—there were riots of anger at the government's noncommunication, followed by riots of terror when the dying outnumbered the liying. Be calm because we know best had been ContiGov's attitude right up until the end— but what it knew had not been sufficient to save the country.

Parric stopped for a brief lunch, and to shake off the bile that contaminated his daydreams and dulled his attention to safety. There was no sense now in rehashing, evaluating, passing Olympian judgment on the dead and those who had survived to pass this way again. Dorin, if nothing else, had taught him that to live by ifs and shoulds was not living at all, but only sleepwalking with your eyes open. Keep it up and you'll eventually break your goddamned neck.

With that, at least, Parric would not argue.

7

So it remained for him to find suitable response to the screaming nightmares that demanded to know why he of all the people left in the world was walking alone to Philayork.

In the beginning, on the first day, he'd told himself it was for revenge.

A scream. Sharp. Brief.

Parric stiffened, his shoulders working to center the pack in case he had to run. Directly ahead at some one hundred meters, the road swerved abruptly to the right, stretched behind dead straight to the mountains' horizon. He dropped to his knees, hands braced, as he listened to the echoes swirl like harpies above him. Shouts, a second scream, and he scrambled up the bank into the underbrush. With a practiced jerk of his torso the pack flipped into his hands. A snap, tug, and the hand weapon he'd stolen from Central's armory fit warmly into his palm. It was a lasered model, pre-Plague rare and too precious for indiscriminate use without a means for recharging. At the same time, his free hand dipped into a sheath near the top of a thigh-high boot and freed the oiled, glittering blade of his balanced dagger. It blurred as he sliced a tunnel through a bush to watch for the people who'd shattered his chances for a full day's walk.

He cursed. Once.

Heard footfalls. Whoever was in the running lead had not taken refuge in the forest. Stupid. With all the traps laid by the road's dilapidation, the woodland would be as much a hindrance to the pursuers as the quarry. He shook his head and cautiously raised himself to peer down the slope. Three figures raced around the bend toward him. They were weaponless, naked, two men and a woman. Even from his awkward position, he could see the crimson shading their feet, the vivid welts scarring their legs and chests.

A dozen paces, and one of the men suddenly pitched forward. His forehead struck a jagged outcropping of tarmac, split and splashed red. The woman stumbled to a halt, yanked at her hair and ran back. Parric gnawed his moustache angrily. The second man paused only for a moment before shouting a single warning and continuing his flight. The woman ignored him, knelt beside the body and touched its back. Her head shook violently. When she rose to run again, however, it was evident something had died with her friend. Her legs barely lifted, her arms dangled at her sides; and as she drew closer, Parric could see her mouth hanging open as though her running would be sufficient to draw in the necessary air.

Her cry was a weak one. A cornered animal too weary to fight.

The second man dropped to his knees directly below Parric. He looked up to the sky, and toppled onto his face. A second later he began crawling. Stopped. Was still.

"Come on," Parric whispered to the woman. "Come on, goddamnit!"

A deeper voice, raised in discovery and elation. Two men dressed in the tightfitting camouflage of Hunters' garb darted around the bend and, seeing the dead man, slowed to a confident walk. They were grinning. One carried a club of polished wood, the other a bulky rifle Parric recognized as an ML-9, a military laser too scarce to have been appropriated by accident.

Parric prayed for a miracle of intervention.

The woman reached the fallen man and tugged at his shoulder helplessly, then pounded on his back in frustration. Her screams had turned hoarse. The pursuers took their time closing in, and Parric wasted little time in moral debate. He stood suddenly and raised his left hand, gripped its wrist with a steadying right. He fired, and the rifleman dropped. The woman's screams subsided to a choking sob as he plummeted down the bank and placed

9

himself, legs apart, beside her. His arms were still extended, and the clubman hesitated.

"Don't," Parric said. The man reached toward his dead companion's weapon. "Leave him be and come over here. Slowly."

"Who are you?" said the woman.

Parric ignored her. He watched only the hand that swung the club, watched the arc lengthen tentatively as the Hunter considered the odds of his survival. Suddenly a fly darted in front of Parric's eyes, seemingly aiming directly into them. He shook his head to clear his vision, and instantly the club was in the air. He threw himself forward beneath its erratic trajectory, firing before he struck the ground, cursing as the man screamed once and collapsed, shaking violently while his hands clawed at his face. He reached out for air, jerked once, was still.

And there were the birds. And the insects. The woman's grief. And a fly that landed on Parric's wrist to preen its black head.

Father, what the hell do you expect to gain by going out there? The glory of dying for a set of boundaries that don't even exist anymore?

I don't expect anything, Orion. Except, maybe, to come back.

Mathew. Let's go find Mathew. Maybe he can talk some sense into you.

I doubt it, son. He has troubles of his own. I think he wants to join the rehab teams, but he doesn't quite know why yet.

Father, the only thing Mathew cares about is his damned dice and the money he owes.

Perhaps.

Willard, then. They may have made him into an old man, damnit, but he still knows the difference between sense and nonsense.

10

Willard was with your Grandfather, Orion. He'll be with me, too.

Damnit, Father, you're going to die!

But not for glory, Orion. There's no glory at all in the act of dying.

Ignoring the stinging at his chest and palms, he pushed himself to his feet and stumbled into the bushes, vomiting until his lungs threatened to collapse and the pain overcame the revulsion at the nausea. A throbbing erupted at the base of his neck. He slumped to his buttocks and gripped his head. Tears salted his lips. He rocked silently, slowly, felt the sun spread a gently warm blanket over the chill that wouldn't quit his spine. Finally, he wiped his face and beard with his loosely puffed shirtsleeves, examined the scrapes on his hands with numbing detachment and, feeling somewhat foolish and angrily embarrassed, returned to the road.

The woman was sitting with her legs straight out before her. The man was still unconscious, his head face up in her lap. Parric looked down at them, frowning, disregarding their nudity as he scanned the unpleasant map of pain etched into their skin. They were young—he guessed close to his own twenty-eight—and thin without seeming starved. Animated corpses, he thought as he retrieved his pack. They said nothing, barely acknowledged his presence as he rummaged for the medkit and began cleansing the open sores, spreading a sweet cooling balm over the mouths of the lesions. They were as children in their mute acceptance of his ministrations, and though he knew he was being rough, they didn't complain. Their silence was unnerving.

When he finished, he shifted onto his haunches and stared at them. The woman, her light brown hair webbed in wet strands across her face, stared back. Suddenly he reached into the pack and pulled out his cloak. She looked

11

at it dumbly until he pushed it into her hands. She held it a moment, then draped it over her shoulders, covering her small breasts and arranging what she could over the man's waist.

Parric swallowed to moisten his throat. "How do you feel?" and knew instantly it was a stupid question.

She sniffed, and he feared her crying again. Bulges appeared and vanished under the mudcolored cloth. Testing my skills, he thought, and waited patiently. Finally, evidently satisfied, she worked at a fleeting smile; and in that instant he saw her face smooth to a fullness that banished the hollows at her cheeks, the angles that unflatteringly squared her nose and chin.

"I'm tired," she said.

Parric nodded. "I wouldn't sleep now, though. There's still the night to come."

"What if we have to run again?"

He glanced at the fallen bodies and cursed his carelessness. He should have checked the road beyond the bend immediately for others. But the woman didn't seem anxious; her question, in fact, seemed more for his benefit than hers.

"Well, I'm not going anywhere," he said finally. "And sleeping or awake, you and he aren't in any condition to do much walking, much less try to outrun guys like that."

Her chin lifted, the defiance out of place. "I'm not afraid to die, you know."

"Good for you. I knew somebody like that once. He died. Personally, I prefer living. It's much more convenient."

She hadn't understood and her expression showed it. Parric considered explaining, brushed it aside and stretched his arms over his head. She followed the movement as though mesmerized, and he saw how heavy her head was on her neck. The muscles were bulging with

12

strain, and he realized for the first time how near to collapse she was.

"Hey," he said, as softly as he could, "don't worry about me, lady. I'm not one of them, and I'm sure as hell not their friend. For that matter, if it'll make you feel any better, I don't even know who they are."

He grinned at the shudder that jerked her upright, and the aftermath: a visible relaxation that eased the lines of her neck and passed the worry from the tension at her mouth. Her hand drifted to her chin, then to the face in her lap, the fingers caressing and avoiding while she traced the blunted features marred by what seemed to Parric to be stings from a whip. Though repelled, he wasn't surprised. When the world had descended into hell and wasn't about to rise on the third, or the thirtieth day, much of the outlying population had fallen under the irresistible influence of local demigogues who had rediscovered medieval traditions of power/force/power that were being nurtured behind walls of fear as unyielding as if they'd been fashioned by master masons. Some had taken titles, others just the rule; and more often than not their activities were restricted to their immediate sectors. It was the exceptions that worried the ContiGov, however. These larger, more ambitious duchies were rapidly becoming serious rivals to Central's leaders whose reluctance to utilize force over reason hampered their efforts in some areas to the brink of desperation.

And in this desperation, Mathew had given up his gambling and his precious dice.

Parric grunted and glanced with disgust at the westering sun. He rose, hefted the sleeping man into his arms and carried him up the slope and into the woods. The woman stared after him, followed, and her whimpers stabbed his back like blades of ice.

Five minutes walking and he stopped, laid the man carefully on a scattering of needles, and set about widen-

13

ing a space for them to sit, and rest. Perspiration blinded him, and he stood often to shake the stinging moisture from brows and beard. And when he'd laid a firebase, he dug into his pack.

"Here," he said, and tossed the woman a pair of trousers tightly bundled. "They won't fit but they'll keep you warm." A second pair, and his last, he pulled onto the man. When he looked up, the woman was weaving broad leaves into slippers she slipped over her bloodied feet and fastened with the roots of a vine.

"I know," she said to his frown. "They'll fall apart as soon as I start walking again. But for now, they'll be cool. And I can at least pretend I'm ready for anything."

"You sound better," he said, truthfully. Her despair was gone, or at least smothered by her attempts to pull back to normality.

"I feel better." She piled leaves and needles expertly into a cushion and sat, her back resting at the side of a weather-round boulder. "Where are you from?"

He pointed toward the sun. "A place. The ContiGov is there."

Her eyes widened, then she shook her head. "I could almost believe anything you told me except that."

"Why not? It's true. A place called Town Central. It was used for experiments with androids and such before the Wind. Now it's home." His laugh was like a fox's bark. "They're trying to put things back together again." He explained, briefly, the rehabs and the crowherds, the continuing work on androids so their acceptance by the general population would be made easier. She listened politely, but asked no questions. "I have this feeling," he said, interrupting himself and lying on his side so he could watch both her and the road, "I have this feeling you don't believe me."

"Should I? I've heard about this place of yours, this Town Central or whatever you call it, but you'll never

14

convince my people that it exists. And even if they believed, they wouldn't care much."

"Oh?" An unreasonable flurry of anger clenched one fist. "And why wouldn't they care? I would think—"

"If ContiGov is still around, it won't have many friends, friend. There are still lots of us who blame it for what happened. And I wasn't even born then."

"Now that's dumb," he snapped without thinking. "The war wasn't their fault, you know. All we got was the fallout, so to speak."

She shrugged and turned to the unconscious man. "He thought there might be something, you know. He said we should try to find it, join it, maybe." Her smile twisted in bitterness. "He also has a big mouth."

"That's why—"

She nodded and hugged herself tightly. "His name is Thomas. Like the man in the story, he doubted too much."

Parric disliked the riddles she posed without speaking, and said so.

"Sorry. It gets to be a habit where we're from." Then she pointed to her throat. "I'm Lynna."

"And I suppose you doubted, too, right?"

What she had done, she explained, was marry Thomas at a time when he was too busy pushing at the status quo of their town, Redlin. Shortly after the Plague Wind had run its course, a number of refugees had drifted into the community, nearly doubling what was left of its population. There had been, according to the stories, confusion, a great deal of fighting, and a manic moratorium on construction of both ideas and accommodations. Anarchy blossomed when the Redlin Council was slaughtered during a food riot. And from that came a man named Wister who organized a defense committee that sprouted instant arms of semilegality. When there was calm, there was Wister.

His rules were simple: outsiders were driven off in fear of the Plague and its ghost, insiders were detained in fear of their leaving.

"He's more afraid of people running out on him than anything else, I think," Lynna said.

"But I don't understand how he keeps control. I mean, surely there must be some of you, enough of you who could make this guy find a hole deep enough to crawl into."

"You make it sound so easy."

"Well, isn't it?"

Her cheeks puffed, deflated, and she said nothing until he pressed her again. "Sure it is. All you have to do is convince the younger ones that life was different, and better, before Wister. Some difference: killing, fighting, every block with its own army, diving for cellars every time a breeze came up." She leaned toward him, her eyes only slightly darker in the shadows of the pine boughs that shifted over their heads. "Are you one of those people who think a democracy is a natural form of politics?"

"You say it like it was a curse, lady."

"Lynna. Have you ever seen a democracy deal with a riot?"

He had a retort, swallowed it, pushed the query aside with a tired wave. His hands were still stinging, and his chest ached where it had thumped against the road. And in remembering, he excused himself curtly and clambered back down the bank.

The club was lying in a pothole, its palm-smoothed handle jutting into the air. He uttered a grunt of surprise when he lifted it, and instantly drove off an image of what he would have resembled had it connected with his skull. It was heavy, far heavier than wood ought to be, and when he checked the rounded tip, he saw the plug of metal. Nice, he thought. Carrying this thing around, that guy must have had an arm like a tree trunk. He turned, spun the

16

club into the shallow ditch between shoulder and bank; it was regrettably too heavy to carry—he had too far to walk and didn't need the extra burden.

A moment of control of his stomach, and he forced himself to drag the bodies off into the brush. Puzzled, then, he stared at the road's curve and wondered why there had been no pursuit.

"So ask the girl, idiot," he muttered; but when he returned to the clearing, Lynna had stretched out at Thomas's side. She raised her head at the sound of his approach, lowered it upon recognition. And he stood over them, shaking his head and wishing he had a polite way of informing them he didn't want their company. He thought they would be fine once they'd had some rest, and if the Wistermen didn't follow too soon. The man Thomas, despite his condition, looked to be a strong one, would probably be formidable with the odds more in his favor. Parric decided to leave them rifle and club, after he'd kept the former beside him for the night. He ran back for it and placed it carefully next to his pack.

Firewood next as he figured two hours more of sun before the mountains drew in the evening, and the chill of starlight.

"Hey," Lynna said sleepily, "would you mind sitting down or something? You're making me nervous."

"Sorry," and he took her seat by the rock. "By the way, my name is Parric. Orion Parric."

There was no response.

"You asleep already?"

"No," she said, and pushed herself up on one elbow, the cloak sliding off one breast until she grabbed at it. Slowly. "I was just thinking."

"Well, stop thinking. If you won't take my advice and wait until nightfall, the least you can do is get some rest. You probably have a long way to go, to get away from this Wister, I mean."

17

She frowned and pushed the straggling hair away from her face. "Orion," she said slowly, as though it had a flavor she was trying to place.

"My father's idea," said Parric. "Not mine."

"Was he shorter than you?"

It was Parric's turn to frown. "Almost a head and a half. He took after his father. I take after nobody. Why?"

"If his name was Dorin," she said quietly, "I think I knew him."

II

THOMAS HAD HAD a session with Wister. For several months, the younger man had been wondering aloud why an exploratory expedition to Philayork hadn't been sent out. It seemed, he contended, the most sensible move to make after half a century. If the city was still working and habitable, many of Redlin's potentially major problems of supply and space would be immediately relieved by a mass migration. And even if the support systems had broken down or the fuel supplies exhausted—neither of which was very likely—the effort would at least enable them to evaluate more accurately the condition of the outside world. There might even be a comsystem that could initiate long range contact with other enclaves.

Wister, not surprisingly, had disagreed. In addition to pointing out the limitless space the mountains provided, he claimed to have witnessed as a child the horrors of the Plague sweeping invisibly through the walkways. His uncompromising descriptions of the panics, the murders, the chaotic carnage when the Guard arrived to restore order and were instead caught up in the terror, were vivid and ultimately convincing.

"He kept on and on," said Lynna, "until there wasn't anyone around who thought Thomas wasn't deliberately trying to lead them into some ghastly form of suicide."

Impatience knotted Parric's nerves. He could not look directly at the woman without having to stem impulses to

19

strangle her. But at the same time, her talking brought color to her cheeks and made the swell of her breasts against the cloak less pathetic, more provocative. Her slim attractiveness reached him, forced him to nod encouragement.

"Dorin," he prompted.

She closed her eyes briefly. Thomas groaned, and an arm thrashed over his head, striking her on the cheek. She yelped, grabbed his wrist and held it down until his tremors subsided. A finger at his brow. "Fever," she said flatly. "He was sick before we left. Wister, you see, was talking about moving into a neighboring town. Hovins. It's deserted, and he wants the empty space for our people. Thomas said he'd need a large army to protect both towns and the land around them. But Wister has this way of looking at you . . ." She rubbed a finger under her nose and searched the sunspotted ground for the words she wanted. "He made it sound like . . . like the destiny of the world depended on Redlin. He kept saying mighty oaks need water to grow from acorns, or something like that."

"I know," Parric said.

"Anyway, he and a man named Shem started training some of the men to fight in case they needed to." Lynna spat dryly. "Fight what? Ghosts? Anyway, Thomas spoke up again. Big mouth, like I said. Right in the middle of a meeting he started shouting about idiots who look for trouble, and stuff like that. Some of the men jumped him. He was beaten and thrown into a cell."

And Wister naturally calmed them down, Parric thought. He reached between his knees and plucked a flowering weed from the earth. The petals were of faded gold, the silken moisture cool between his fingers. The situation was rapidly becoming ridiculous. The more Lynna talked, the more he felt a restraint on his mission snaking around his legs. But his discontent stemmed more

20

from resignation than frustration: it had been that way most of his adult life, the plans made that grew out of control and forced him to actions he hadn't even considered possible. It was as though he was an animal racing for freedom across a meadow, and crashing abruptly and painfully against a barrier that sprang out of the air and shoved him onto a new course. And it wasn't the stopping that angered him—it was the not knowing which way he was being herded.

Lynna asked for a drink of water. Parric touched his dry lips to the back of a hand, then grabbed a container from his pack and made his way deeper into the woods toward a stream he'd heard while he was carrying Thomas. When he returned, the man was sitting up, propped against the trunk of a winterbent sapling.

"You knew Dorin," he said. No thanks for his life, no supplications of libations for Parric's godlike intrusion. The voice was hard. Rising from a dead space.

"I knew him," Parric said, handing over the water and squatting by the rock again. "He was my father."

If he expected a sudden explosion of emotion, a release of the peculiar tension that filled the makeshift clearing and pressed more heat into the sun than previously had been, he was disappointed. Thomas only nodded, taking small sips of the cool liquid and holding them several seconds in his mouth before swallowing. Lynna waited her turn.

"She," said Parric, pointing to the woman, "was telling me about your Wister."

"No more heart than a goddamned andy," Thomas said.

"You should have kept your mouth shut," Parric said. "You might have been able to do more on the quiet than jumping around like a squirrel with its tail on fire."

"Did she tell you that?"

Parric scowled. "Lynna did, yes," he said, coming

21

down hard on her name. "But not in so many words."

"Thomas, he's Dorin's son, remember?"

"I am," Parric said, "and I want to know how you know him. Did he come through here? Maybe three years ago?"

"Yes," Lynna said when Thomas refused to answer. "He's dead."

She stared at her hands, but only Thomas bit at his lips. "Tell him," he muttered.

"He came through with a number of other men. In March, I think it was."

"Possibly," Parric said, quickly checking a mental calendar. "He wanted to get to Philayork before summer so . . . he could get back home before winter set in."

"He stayed only a little while. I didn't talk to him much. I met him, see, because I was . . . well, I was on the unofficial reception committee. He spent a lot of time with Wister. I don't know why. I wasn't told what they said. He stayed . . . how long, Tom?"

Thomas was plucking disdainfully at his narrowed trousers. They were loose at the calves for comfort, coolness and warmth, but it was apparent he wasn't familiar with their design. Parric tried not to grin; the expansion of his own, black pair was hidden, tucked into his boots.

"Thomas!"

"Three or four days, okay? I only saw him from a distance." He was sullen, and Parric had the distinct impression that he was afraid of Lynna. "I never got to talk with him."

"I don't believe you," Parric said.

Lynna tried to look shocked, and Thomas glared, like a sulking child.

"Come on," Parric said, accentuating his disgust. "Listen, if you were so damned hot to get the hell out, there was no possible way you would stay away from him.

22

He was going to Philayork. You knew it. You wanted to go. I want to know what he said."

"Nothing."

"He said he wouldn't take Thomas with him," Lynna whispered.

A flash of blue and grey broke through the foliage and landed a hand's breadth from Parric's foot. He watched as the bird tilted its head from side to side, cocked it steady, then flew off, as silently as it had arrived. Perspiration dampened the back of his billowing green shirt, and he felt for the first time the press of the late afternoon's heat through the leaves. There was no breeze.

Come with me, Orion.
No.
You might learn something.
I've learned enough. And don't look at me that way.
What way?
That way. Stop it!
Whatever you say, son. Are you sure you won't change your mind?
Never, and don't say never is too long to talk about.
I wasn't going to say it.
No, but you were thinking it.

There are too many facades here, Parric thought as he rose to relieve the stiffness in his thighs. She talks and learns nothing, and he talks and finds out he can't go to his damned heaven. And there's something else. He wants to say it; she won't let him.

"He told me he didn't want to lead a caravan."

"He didn't put it that way," Lynna said, sneering. "What he said, Orion," and though she looked at him, her comments were still directed to her husband, "what he said was that he didn't want to attract a lot of attention to

23

himself. All he was going to do was take a look around and then report back to wherever he had come from."

"And he didn't tell you where he was from?"

She bridled at the disbelief in his question. "No! And I didn't ask! He was going to look at what had survived in the city. He didn't want to attract unpleasant company."

"Hunters," Parric said. "Quasi soldiers of small towns who don't like strangers."

"I guess so," she said when he cast a glance back toward the road. "Anyway, he promised Thomas he would tell him what he'd seen. If it was safe to go there, I mean."

Parric waited. If Thomas had just been released from his confinement, if he had contracted something while there, he obviously wouldn't have been in any condition to make the trip. Dorin was no fool when it came to details like that. Only in the overview. Thomas was suffering from little more than hurt pride.

"But what about this Wister?" he asked. "Didn't he tell anyone anything?"

"Shem, probably, but no one else that I know of," Lynna said, again filling the silence when her husband refused to speak. "He just acted like he thought your father was a little crazy, wandering around the outside like that. He . . . humored him, I guess the word is. There was a dinner the night they left. Everyone drank a lot, and there was music and things, and then Dorin and the old man—"

"Old man?"

She nodded. "Didn't you know him? There was this old man with him." She laughed her puzzlement. "They were always together. Visiting some of the houses, walking through the streets. Was he a relation or something?"

"Or something," Parric said.

"He never said much," Thomas said. "Just would look

24

at you like he was trying to decide if you were worth talking to. Strange. I didn't like him much.''

"That's because you didn't know him,'' Parric said.

And suddenly he was tired and then angry because there was no reason for him to feel that way. Part of it, he knew, was the way the couple spoke about his father, as though he was merely an interesting character who had passed through on his way to someplace few people cared about. The dispassionate manner of their conversation grated, an impersonal abrasive that made him want to grab for the nearest tree and yank it out by the roots.

It was irrational, and he muttered an excuse about nature's call before thrashing noisily through the brush to get away from them.

For a while, then, he hated them. Personifications of what he decided was a multileveled guilt. A worrisome sense of responsibility because he hadn't gone with Dorin, hadn't been there to perhaps try to save his life when it needed saving. The notion that if Willard couldn't do it, no one could, was neither comforting nor convincing. There might have been something he could have done.

And again: revenge. He claimed to be a sensitive man, a sensible man who considered his options and took only the one that tipped the scale toward dying of old age. Revenge, however, was definitely not a sensible reaction, even if it was predictable. Guilt, then, about his own shortcomings, and the possibility that he wasn't nearly as in control of himself as he'd trained himself to be.

Yet again: that something else. A faint, unformed nagging that underlay and somehow hinted at superseding all the rest. It was the stuff of his nightmares. Like the threatening spectre of maddened androids whose biomechanisms had been unbalanced by the Plague.

He leaned against a twisted oak and began shredding the leaves from a low-hanging branch. The world was getting complicated again. He needed silence. He looked for a symbol in the forest, a talisman, a sign from somewhere to reset his mind and drive the extraneous back into oblivion.

What there was, however, was a scream, an angrily surprised shout, and he plunged back through the underbrush toward the camp. Wister's men, he thought as he bent to free a blade from its sheath. It was only a matter of time before his stupidity caught up with him. Allowing them to rest comfortably while those dead soldiers' mates began wondering, searching, finding, and setting out to complete the assignment. A branch slapped at his face. He ducked, stumbled, reached out to snatch a handful of laurel to keep him on his feet.

Ahead, through the green-tinted light, he saw Lynna's hair bobbing as though she was ducking from thrown missiles. Thomas wasn't to be seen, but sounds of thrashing and explosive grunts of pain pinpointed his position. Parric slowed, crouched lower, turned the dagger until the blade settled into his palm. He hefted it in mimed practice.

Then he rose and took the last dive through the edge of the clearing.

It came to him in fragments.

Lynna: dancing frantically out of the way of two men wrestling wildly on the ground.

Forest shrapnel: leaves, needles, stalks, gouts of earth churning into the dust-filled air.

Thomas: his trousers already shredding like strips of black skin.

Parric ignored Lynna's screamed instructions, sorting out instead the confusion of his hesitation. The attacker was naked. His face temporarily hidden in Thomas' shoulder. His hands raking blood from Thomas's spine.

Lynna ran to him and pushed, but Parric shoved her away while he looked for an opportunity to throw the knife. Suddenly, Thomas was on the bottom, a hand vised at his throat. The dagger shifted, and Parric leapt onto the attacker's back. He snaked an arm around his neck and yanked back, simultaneously thrusting the blade into his side.

Nothing happened.

Thomas broke his head free and screamed, his eyes already bloodshot, bubbles of red froth covering his lips and chin. A fist was raised. Parric released his weapon and grabbed at the wrist, hoping to pull the arm back rapidly enough to break it.

Straining.

The intruder reached up and held Parric's bicep. Without turning around. Parric yelped as he was lifted from the ground, over a shoulder, came to rest at the clearing's edge. His mouth opened, gulping, and he arced to flip himself onto his stomach. He shook his head to clear it and felt claws tugging at his arms. Lynna was shouting something into his ear, and he slapped a palm over it before he was deafened.

He stared, gaping.

It was a Rogue, its hands encasing Thomas's skull, lifting and slamming into the dirt. There was no resistance.

It was a Rogue, its hands around the neck of a man who had no breath left to scream.

Parric touched the streak in his hair.

His first impulse was to run, to grab the girl and run back to Central. Lynna slapped him. He spat. She slapped him again. He stood, shaking, searching the campsite desperately until he saw his pack and the dull gleaming beside it. He had never used a rifle, wouldn't know how to activate it, but there were other ways. So his grandfather had said.

"Behind the tree," he ordered, and lunged for the rifle, lifting it by its barrel. The Rogue saw him. Stood over Thomas's body like an animal protecting its kill. Its face had no lines to give it an age, was only smeared with a

27

mixture of dirt and blood not its own. The torso and legs were gouged. Its mouth opened, and the sounds that rumbled toward him were less words than snarls. Parric took a step back, and the Rogue lifted its arms like battering rams and charged.

Lynna screamed.

Parric ducked to one side and swung the rifle, his hands snapping numb as metal struck the heavy casing at the android's hips. Momentum carried it into a bush. It tilted sideways, and fell. A hand poked through leaves as though air would pull it upright.

Parric backed toward the road, shifting the rifle from hand to hand so he could flex the sting from his fingers. A flash of white, and he could hear Lynna circling behind him.

"The ditch," he shouted suddenly. "Lynna, get the club in the ditch!"

Then he turned and ran, letting the android's pursuit serve to ignite his adrenalin. And further: the sight of his dagger uselessly embedded in its unfeeling back.

There was no sense in trying to outrun it. Lynna's injured feet would soon slow them down, and they would be hunted, stalked, driven to ground within hours and butchered as that family had been. And he was too close now to allow a mechanized parody of a godwish stop him.

The ground sloped, and he slowed until his footing adjusted to keep him from plunging headfirst into the open. He leapt through a gap and landed on hands and knees on the other side of the ditch. Lynna ran to him, the club held in both her hands.

"It's too heavy," she said, and there was an instant's understanding that this time, and not before, she was afraid.

Parric battled the confusion, then turned to watch the Rogue moving slowly toward them. It had no sense of

28

place, or of time, no compulsions of urgency. It was its own tragic weakness, but more than offset by the terror its simple existence created.

"All right," he said, curiously calm. "Take this," and he exchanged rifle for wood. "When he gets close enough, use it like a sword and go for its eyes."

She blinked her puzzlement and he snatched the rifle back impatiently. He gripped it with both hands and jabbed at the air until she nodded quickly. Then he took up the club and sidled away, drawing the android to him. It stumbled into the ditch, climbed and stood silent for a moment; the only sound was the rasping air that passed through Parric's clenched teeth.

It moved.

Clumsily, at first, over the gaps in the road, then with more assurance as Parric stood his ground. Lynna stayed just behind it, moving in until she could leap suddenly to its side. The barrel lunged into its left eye. There was a roar of surprise, and the glitter of silver shards spraying from its face. As it spun, half-blinded, Parric raised the club over his shoulder and ran forward, using his momentum for additional power, nearly leaving the ground as he swung and felt the casing give on impact. The android went down on one knee. Parric swung again before it could stand. Lynna, quick to the example, reversed the rifle and pounded the android wildly, more often than not missing, but preventing the Rogue from finding a balance.

She struck a shoulder and its right arm dangled uselessly. A swing that took her in a complete circle shattered the right lens, and the Rogue's face contorted as it lifted toward the sun.

She grinned, and dropped the rifle. "He's safe."

Parric walked up behind it. "No," he said as it turned clumsily to his voice. "I've heard stories." Methodically, then, and trying to keep an intruding image of Willard from superimposing itself over the Rogue's inhuman face, he smashed at the hips until the casing split, the brain/heart/core was exposed. And he destroyed it.

In silence.

They buried Thomas beneath a cairn. There had been rumors that wolves from the north were making their way into the mountains; but they were rumors only, born of half-remembered hopes that not everything had been eliminated by the Wind. Parric waited on the road until Lynna had found an expression of farewell. When she rejoined him, her eyes were dry and he said nothing.

Walking, then, with the sun at their backs. He stripped a birch and fashioned crude sandals for her, and gave her a shirt she immediately fastened to the neck. She refused to allow him a check of the medication.

They passed the remains of a landcar, upended and rusted, and swarming with ants.

Weeds, grass, and struggling young trees formed islands in the roadbed. Another fifty years, he thought, and no one will know.

An hour toward sunset, and Lynna tugged at his arm.

"Are you taking me back?"

He shook his head. "I'm not taking you anywhere. I have a place to get to." He glanced pointedly at her feet. "And you're hardly in any shape to keep up with me."

"Where?"

"A place, okay? A place."

Another ten paces, and she was tugging again.

"I'm not afraid to go back, you know."

He couldn't help a smile. "You're stubborn, I'll say that. And you don't seem to be afraid of anything, do you?"

Her hair was draped over one shoulder, long enough to touch her stomach. She stroked it close to her breasts. "I only ran with him because he was my husband. I was only scared because I ran. If I go back now, the worst I can get is a screaming scolding."

He didn't doubt it. No matter what else she might be—might have been in this curious town of Redlin—she was still a woman. Childbearing. The fact that the soldiers, Hunters, whatever they had been, had even killed a man was testimony enough to Wister's strength. Next to the preservation of insect-controlling birds, man was the resource most jealously guarded in a world Parric thought better for the shortage.

"Who was the other man?" he asked.

"A friend of his. No one important. He won't be missed all that much."

He. His. My husband. Not Thomas, nor were there tears at his mention. And who won't be missed? Thomas, or the friend?

"What would happen to me if I took you back?"

She looked at him steadily. "I don't know."

"Is it far from here?"

"We could make it just after noon tomorrow." There was nothing in her voice that carried thanks, hope, or a fear of her return. They could have been talking about a change in the weather.

She puzzled him. All of it, in fact, puzzled him and presented a temptation he felt less and less able to deny. A man named Thomas is thrown into a cell for preaching expansion. Released, he talks with Dorin who refuses to take him to Philayork. Another cell, presumably for the same offense. Why was he released a second time? Escape? If so, why the friend and the wife? It was possible, though not very likely, that they had been jailed also. No. Not Lynna. This woman who kept pace with his long strides despite her makeshift footgear was something more than a female to be coddled because of her potential. He allowed his eyes to close several seconds: an image of her as she'd been sitting on the road beside Thomas's unconscious form. And again at the clearing. Her stomach was flat, her breasts firm—no signs of the stretching, the slight, telltale sagging bearing a child tracked across a body. Yet, she was easily his age. And the slender frame was thin by design, not deprivation.

"I think," she said, and he blinked comically at her interruption, "I think Wister would probably not do anything. Not at first, anyway. He'd be too interested in you. You did save me from the Rogue, you know. That should count for something, don't you think?"

"He sounds like a man with a heart," Parric said sourly. He shifted the club from right shoulder to left, beginning to regret not taking the rifle instead. But its barrel and butt had been thumped out of shape, and minus the tools for repair, the club was now the more valuable.

"He has plans," she said.

"You told me. Hovins, right?" He was beginning to dislike the carrots she pulled from the air.

"No. Something else."

Forget it, he thought. I don't like the bait.

They crossed a bridge immense in its expenditure of concrete and steel. Hovercats and landcars were tangled along its entire length, and Parric kept to the molded railings so not to confirm what his imagination scattered through the lifeless hulks. Below, a chasm, and a river reflecting the sky that had shaded to a deep, depthless blue. Shadows laced from bank to bank. A patch of white water seemed frozen in the distance. The contrast stirred him. More so because he thought there should not have been a reason for it. Destruction ahead, creation behind. Below. Around. He nodded to himself, thinking the odds were just about right.

In favor of the grass.

She asked him if he'd made up his mind. "I can show you a way around it, if you don't want to go with me."

"I'm not afraid," he said.

"Nobody said you were."

"I just have something to do."

"You've already said that."

At the far end of the bridge, he stopped and reached up to hang onto a pylon. She stood in front of him, watching. It was apparent she didn't care one way or the other, and he couldn't help wondering what kind of a wife she'd been to a husband like that. She smiled, then, and raised an eyebrow in a question almost mocking.

"Just for the sake of argument," he said, "what would you have done if I had left you back there?"

The mockery left her face. "That sounds like you think you are taking me with you. You're not, you know. I could turn around and leave any time I wanted to. Find another town. There's got to be another one around someplace that's inhabited."

Again, she smiled just this side of bemusement, and Parric was reminded of an unpleasantly similar device used by his mother to get either he or his brother to make up their minds to do what she wanted. Rebellion surged, to be contrary battered against the temptation of her intrigue.

But there was still Dorin. And Philayork. And the man who killed the one while ghosting the other.

"This Town Central," she said, abruptly changing the subject, "does it have a lot of people?"

He shrugged.

"Hundreds? Thousands?"

He shrugged again.

"Maybe Dorin told Wister about it. What do you think?"

The relevance eluded him. He turned suddenly, and stared down at the banks of the river. She moved to his side quietly, and he felt her searching for what he was hearing.

You couldn't save him, could you, old man?

No. There were too many.

Come on, Will, you know me better than that. You went out there ready to take care of an army, for crying out loud. How many could there have been? Hundreds?

No.

Fifty? Forty? Two Dozen? Come on, old man, damnit, say more than six words at a time, will you?

Two dozen. Maybe less.

I don't believe it.

Don't.

Damnit, Will, you've brought two corpses back to this hole! And you don't even act like you care!

As much as I can, I do, Orion.

Then how the hell could you have let him be killed? Will, for God's sake, why was he killed?

They were waiting, Orion.

Waiting?

We didn't know their numbers until it was too late.

Have you seen Mathew?

I've told him.

What does he say?

Talk to Orion.

Lynna placed a hand gently, carefully, on his arm. "What are you thinking?"

Parric leaned on the club, used it as a pivot to face her. "I'm thinking maybe if I don't get killed first, I'd kind of like to talk to this man Wister."

"You'll like him," she said. "You really will."

But when she reached out to touch the streak in his beard, he slapped her hand away.

III

By MIDNIGHT, Parric was chafing.

He lay, swaddled in his cloak, staring at the dying fire, hoping the periodic eruptions of short-lived sparks would serve as an hypnotic tranquilizer for his nerves. Lynna, refusing to share his cover—and refusing to take it from him—was asleep, and had been from the moment her head touched the pillow of her arms. He envied her. Having once decided to push into Redlin, he'd become anxious and fearful that something would happen to vanish the town or shorten his life. He wanted to hurry, but Lynna's feet were still too tender for her to stay with him for long. He'd been forced, then, to stop shortly after sunset and set up a camp, and bathe her soles with a thick layer of balm. She kept telling him to relax, laughing, but a drive had been switched on and he was helpless to contain it.

A shift of his shoulders jabbed a stone into his back. He grunted, inched closer to the fire and stared up through the leaves at the stars.

He hated them. All of them. They were smug in their sweep, unending in number, and they contained somewhere in their midst a huge metal pod. Mankind in microcosm. A starship. *The* starship. The *Alpha*. It was part of the familial religion his grandfather had founded. He'd struggled to keep things alive, to restore and rebuild so the men of the *Alpha* would not have made their journey for nothing. Dorin had believed it: a lifetime to order, a barrier to chaos. Orion had scoffed and called it another dream.

And then: his name. In full sunlight he carried the stars with him. A barbed banner draped across his soul. Orion. Hunter. The implications were too obvious, and even in conversation his friends quickly learned to call him Parric.

The stars. If nothing else, Philayork would have lights, and those lights would blot out the constellations and give his nights peace.

He thought of Wister when a cloud shuttered the sky. He laughed, silently. It was a step. The first letter in vengance if his suspicions were correct. He was moving now toward something he could count on, something that would broaden into a dimension where he could move and plan and strike the first blow. His hands fisted at his stomach and rubbed against his shirt in tight spastic circles. He considered crawling out of his cocoon and over to Lynna. He would touch her, kiss the ice that was hidden beneath her lips, tear open the trousers that were his and relieve his celibate anger. But it would be something less than rape, and he refused to believe it was the only way he could take her. Later, he told himself, when her gratitude for rescue sought an outlet more promising than a careful shake of his hand. It would come. People were like that. They had to divest themselves of real or imagined debts quickly or they caused themselves a suffering as artificial as it was insincere. Later. In Redlin.

He slept without knowing his eyes had closed, aware only that suddenly there was sun on his lids, seeing only the pink shades of light that vanished when he sat up. He rubbed at his face, shared his meal, checked Lynna's feet once before following her to the road. She didn't say a word.

"How soon?" he demanded an hour into the sun.

She was moving as jauntily as her aches would allow,

casting glances back over her shoulder and grinning inanely.

For a woman who's going to get hell heaped on her, Parric thought, she definitely doesn't behave like she's repentant.

The road widened further, and its parallel shadow moved up to join it. Great flocks of birds, more than he'd seen in his life, wheeled and screamed overhead. A small brown creature scuttled from den to road, stopped and dashed back. Cloud islands reflected blackly over the forested hills, a breeze skating behind.

A massive upheaval forced them to a detour, and as they thrashed through the woods, Parric realized how much he'd come to depend on the man-made road.

Finally, after a luncheon Parric made them eat while they walked, Lynna stopped and waited for him to catch up.

"All right," she said. "There's a trail off to the right around that far bend. There might be some guards, I don't know. But whatever you do," and she kicked lightly at his boot-tops, "keep those hidden or you'll never get to see Wister."

He nodded, but held on to her shoulder when she turned to lead on. "One question," he said. "And one straight answer. Who the hell are you? I mean, what's all this you're doing?"

"I'm not doing anything," she answered, eyes wide. "You want to see Wister, and I'm going home. What more is there?"

"You didn't answer my question."

"I'm Lynna," she said into his stare. "Lynna Wister."

He thought he should have been startled, but he wasn't. There was too much the toughness of a woman used to leading about her. Small wonder she wasn't killed. And with one question answered, there arose two dozen more.

37

He only asked one: "If you are who you say you are, why did you run?"

She shrugged, and he felt an unpleasant flutter in his stomach. And relief that he hadn't shown her all the contents of his pack.

The guards were sitting under an evergreen. An arc of some forty meters radius had been painstakingly cleared from the tree to the edge of the road, giving them an unobstructed field of view, and fire. They were four, young, their Hunters' uniforms new but ill-fitting. When they saw Lynna and Parric approaching, they took their time getting to their feet, made no moves at all toward the projectile rifles stacked against the tree. Parric kept the club resting casually on his shoulder, but they ignored him, smiling instead at Lynna who waved and called them by name. One pulled a small comlink from his hip pocket and spoke briefly into it.

The unofficial welcoming committee prepares, Parric thought.

"Hot," Lynna said.

"It's not so bad," the one named Anton said. "You get used to it." He nudged the young man standing immediately next to him. "It beats working the cattle, that's for sure."

There seemed to be no difference between them, and Parric frowned. He didn't think he'd know them again, definitely would not be able to pick them out of a crowd. A mold had cast them full grown into the Hunter's green-and-brown coloration that splotched their clothing and tight-fitting skull caps. They even leered alike at Lynna's figure beneath the man's clothes. Segment of an army, and Parric wondered just what Wister was planning on the other side of the hill.

A minute's further bantering, and Lynna led him to a road curiously flat and obviously cleared off within the year. No saplings broke the ground, no winter's surge had yet punched rocks through the well-traveled pathway. It pushed up through the trees, and great ropes of root dangled naked from the roughly cut bank.

"Why didn't you introduce me?" Parric said when they'd passed out of sight.

"Why?" she said. "They don't care as long as you're with me."

Maybe they don't, he thought, but I sure as hell do. He spent the next silent hour puffing up an incline, nearly trotting along a plateau. All the while, he searched the unraveling forest around him, looking for landmarks in case he had to leave faster than Dorin. But there was nothing to see but unending trees and the shrubs that clustered around them. No homes or fortifications, no other guard stations but the one they'd encountered. The mark of a confident man, he thought, or a frightened one.

Finally, the bulk of the hill lay to his right, and the road began a careful descent. He wished, suddenly, that it was winter and the foliage gone so he could see the landscape ahead, and judge for himself the size of the valley they were entering.

Lynna, he noticed, had abruptly started limping more than her injuries warranted.

He grinned. Tough she may be, but certainly not stronger than the man he was about to meet.

The road dipped sharply and swerved between twin boulders as high as any house in Town Central. A second drop, a second curve to the left, and the earth became covered with the smooth newness of black ferroglas paving.

No wonder, Parric thought as he turned to look behind him. The trail's engineering had been completed decades before; all Wister had done was dig up the tarmac.

Rapidly, now, the trees took on an ordered array. Underbrush was gone, and in its place were houses. Small, square, shingled and unpainted for the most part. Greying, browning in the face of the weather. They were spread apart to relieve the sensation of crowding, but they seemed tinier for it, and huddling in on themselves like children ducking from nightmares in corners. There were blocks, street lamps on filigree poles, sculptured shrubbery that defied the history of the world outside. Children in rainbow bright singlets played unfamiliar games in constantly shifting clutches; once in a while an adult, sitting on a porch, standing on a lawn, looked up and stared. But there were no greetings, and Lynna didn't seem to expect any. She kept to the street's center.

"Are you as scared as I am?" she said softly.

"You told me I had nothing to be afraid of," he said, grinning at the angry look she gave him.

"You don't, maybe," she said, "but then you don't have to explain everything to Wister."

"What's to explain? Those troops back there didn't seem surprised, or even concerned, that you had a visitor."

It was a question she wouldn't answer. Her silence suited him, however. He wasn't sure, now, how he would take another one of her revelations. That she had so off-handedly tossed him her name—and by implication, her status—had made him decide it was all part of an exercise she was performing; the best he could do was settle down beside her and watch for his cues.

Five more blocks, and the street suddenly split to square itself around an orderly park centered by a low white building. It was a full fifty meters long with a mansard roof, single story and opaque narrow windows that warned of a warren inside. The solitary door at the front was framed by elaborate pillars that pretended to support a triangular wooden canopy over a porch barely wider than the door itself. A man sat on the topmost of three steps.

Lynna stumbled, and Parric took her shoulder.

The man stood. He was wearing a belted tunic over trousers that appeared to belong to a man half again his size—both were a startling red, as though he'd showered in blood. He waited, then held out a hand to catch the girl when she twisted from Parric's grip and ran forward to hug him.

Touching, Parric thought, and looked away from the homecoming at houses no different than he'd already seen, at people in a variety of dress whose destinations or preambulations did not include passing by their leader. There was life in this town, but not the kind he felt would make him welcome. A tension, rather, like fabric drawn tightly over a too-large frame, a blade here, a strong gust there and it would shred, snap, slap down those who tried to get out of its way. He reached behind him for a reassuring adjustment of his pack. And waited.

When Lynna was finally allowed to rest on the porch— with, Parric noted, no hint of the terrible scolding she'd forecast for herself—a woman opened the door and hurried subserviently to her side. She wore a simple white dress and was barefoot. Lynna ignored her.

"Orion Parric."

Parric nodded and held out a hand, moving it slowly, palm upward. "You're Wister, I take it."

"I am." The voice was high, doubling the unpleasant combination of twang and whine. The man was old and carried his age well. His black hair had not turned, and only his face betrayed the sixty or seventy years that had finally pulled at the pouches under his eyes, the loosening skin at jaw and neck. He held his head tilted slightly toward his left shoulder as though the upraised ear was listening to sounds on the wind. His hand, as Parric shook it, was firm but not strong, and beneath the tunic were bulges that suggested a man well fed and ill exercised.

41

He was a good deal shorter and Parric knew instantly that he did not appreciate having to look up, especially at a stranger.

"You've come a long way," Wister said. "How would you like something to eat? Substantial, I mean."

A hand went unconsciously to Parric's stomach, and he nodded.

"Inside, then, and don't mind the mess."

Inside, Parric thought, was almost fanatically clean. He passed through the front door into an entrance hall that vaulted to the ceiling. Benches lined the paneled walls, carpets seemed to float above the polished floors. Several doors opened onto the transection and through them passed a constant, light stream of human traffic. Local Hunters, women, men in ordinary clothing. All carrying folders and other paraphernalia of a minor bureaucracy. There were children, too, darting about in silent games.

"It's sort of a communal house," Wister explained as they walked toward the rear of the building. "We have our meetings in here, and the various groups within the community use it for their parties and gatherings of a business nature. We have our bank here, funerals, weddings, just about everything you can think of that a town like Redlin needs."

Parric grunted noncommittally. He watched the deference given the man, and in some cases a nervous avoidance of having to greet him. Everything, he thought, just where the old man can keep an eye on things. A baronial hall.

They turned left into a corridor that paced the back of the building. It was quieter here, with no official-looking traffic.

"My quarters," Wister said simply.

A door at the corridor's far end opened before they reached it, and a woman stepped out to greet them. She was Wister's duplicate with the single exception of her hair, which was white, long, and braided to drape over her shoulder. She smiled thinly as Wister made the introductions. Her name was Lilly, her voice was quiet, and Parric tried not to flinch at the distrust evident in her eyes.

Her hand was cold, and she disengaged immediately and followed them into a large sitting room well appointed and dominated by a comunit that had been installed along the back wall. Three youngsters in their early teens were squatting in front of it, watching a program of costumed Eurecom elegance.

"Tapes," Wister explained quickly. "We have the power, luckily, because of a plant Redlin had had installed just before the Wind. The tapes we found on a trip we made not so long ago. It keeps the kids out of trouble." As though the remark were a signal, the trio turned and nodded, obviously hoping they wouldn't be expected to perform feats of conversation. Parric grinned as he passed, but they only stared and returned to their viewing.

A short hallway brought them next to a room at the building's left rear corner. Another living area, but this more in tune with adult pleasures. A chromed barkeep, a smaller comunit grey faced in nonoperation, a scattering of Romanesque lounging couches, and a massive, single-paned window that overlooked the park filling the rest of the square. While Lilly bustled at the 'keep for drinks and shouted into several coms at once for servings of hot food, Parric stood watching the children at play under the ancient trees. Here was the town's heart: beyond the well-tended park he could see glimpses of storefronts and heavier concentrations of pedestrians.

"A normal day," Wister said, coming up behind him. "We haven't let the tragedy get us down."

"Admirable," Parric said without sarcasm. It was. Outside the city complexes, there had been few places like Redlin left in the country; they'd been absorbed, abandoned, deserted for the glitter of Walkways and Hives. And what few there were, were fewer after the Wind. Parric had seen them, too many of them reverting to near savagery before the struggling ContiGov moved in. Filth had been the order. And murder—for food, clothes, the right to a woman's thighs. Redlin, however, had managed to survive. And more.

A meal, then, that Parric ate unashamedly fast. But he had almost forgotten the aromas that freshly cooked meat and hot soft bread could muster—the sweet, bitter, tantilizingly sour tastes that had never been able to permeate the nutrient sticks he carried in his pack. It lay now in a corner behind the couch he had chosen, and he glared at it once as though the look were sufficient punishment for his deprivation.

Refreshment next was in the form of a local ale that was black and tart and forced him to swallow carefully lest his head balloon and send him through the ceiling. The tankard was of polished wood, and he held it gently in both hands, his palms stroking its smooth cool sides.

There was no talk. Meals were apparently a serious affair, and he was glad for it. It allowed him to watch Wister, as he stuffed himself with twice the portions his wife consumed, and the women who served them—frail, silent, setting plates and cups, silverware and tankards in front of him as though there was nothing more they would rather do with their lives. There were four of them, and one Parric recognized as the girl who had fussed over Lynna. She was dully blonde and thin, her hands red, her face pinched from lack of padding beneath her skin. She was in fact a direct contrast to the others, and he wondered why she denied herself vanity.

He tried a smile, but at her sharp, short-lived scowl, knew it made him seem condescending.

After the meal, he forgot her. Lynna had returned, exchanging his clothes for a black-and-gold-striped shift

44

that reached only to the center of her thighs. She reclined on a couch in front of the window, bathed, perfumed, coiffed almost comically, and said nothing at all while Wister spread himself sighing in an old-fashioned armchair. It gave him the advantage. Parric was forced to remain on his backless couch, either reclining or sitting with his hands folded in his lap. He tried both ways and, finally, slid to the floor and used the furniture for a backrest.

"So," Wister said, scratching at his scalp. "Do you mind if we talk?"

Parric shrugged. "You're the host, and I'm grateful for the food. It's the best I've had in . . . in a long time."

"Your pleasure pleases me," Wister said. "Now, Lynna tells me you're related to a visitor we had a couple of years or so back. She said you were his son."

Guile enticing guile. The Redlin leader's face was disquieting in its passivity.

"His eldest," Parric said.

Wister unaccountably smiled. "I remember him vaguely. Not too tall, correct? Said he was on his way to Philayork for some reason or other."

The pause was Parric's to fill, but he only nodded.

"And you?"

"The same."

"Why?"

The answer was quick. "I want the men who killed him."

Wister leaned back in his chair and folded his hands across his chest. "I'm sorry," he said. "Lynna neglected to mention that last to me." He promptly sent a wrist-slapping scowl in her direction, but she wasn't looking. "I didn't know he'd died. How did it happen?"

"Ambush. They had reached the city Hive and were attacked unexpectedly. One man escaped."

Wister frowned. "He was lucky, then. It was a dangerous trip. I told your father that, you know. I told him there were stories about the city and what it contains. Scavengers, raiders, people turned into no better than rats who wait to prey on such as him. He shouldn't have gone.''

"He thought he had to,'' Parric said quietly.

''And do you think the same thing? That you have to go there and kill the men who killed your father? I thought you would have had better things to do with your time than to make a wasteful trip.''

Lilly returned with a glass tray laden with tankards. She offered one to Wister, who tasted the liquid, nodded and watched as she gave one to Lynna, herself, Parric last—a deliberate insult for which no one apologized. Parric used the moment to break away from the old man's stares and look at the reflection of his eyes in the ale. The conversation had turned into a catechism, Parric supplying the answers to questions perfunctorily asked. He decided Wister need not know more.

"Yes,'' he finally said. "And no.''

Wister gaped, then glanced at his daughter and laughed —loudly, while Parric smothered his frown in a swallow of ale.

"Listen,'' the old man said, "you're quite right to snap at me like that. Here I am prying instead of hosting, while you are tired from your journey and probably wishing I would shut up and leave you to rest.''

He stood, emptied his tankard and waited while Parric struggled to his feet. Then he took his arm and the two walked back to the front door. "Humor me just a while longer,'' he said as they descended the steps. "Let me show you around just a little. Then you can go to your quarters—which need a little cleaning up anyway—and forget all about me.''

He looked into Parric's face, his eagle's head cocked sharply, and Parric shrugged half-hearted agreement. It wasn't quite as rude as Lilly's snub, but it sufficed to redden Wister's face. He turned on his heel and led the way around the building and across the parkland to what was clearly the main thoroughfare. Here Parric saw the shops he'd spotted earlier, the pedestrians who rushed, lounged, stared frankly or ignored him completely. There was no motorized traffic, and Parric wondered: Wister did not seem the kind of man who would allow 'cats or landcars to fall into disrepair, unless, of course, they were reserved for the new aristocracy. They passed quickly through a residential area whose houses were roofed with the neat black rectangles of solar cells, and through a second street of shops over which mingled the odors of newly cut crops and the stench of freshly butchered cattle. A turn again, and they were strolling along a street that led directly back to the central square.

They stopped at a corner, and Wister pointed to the faint glinting sunset reflected in the waters of a small lake, muttering something Parric couldn't understand about fish and survival.

Then he leaned against a tree, and in the shadows of the leaves that laced across his face, Parric saw the true age Wister tried to conceal. Such an age, Parric thought, that required assistance, and he had yet to meet or even hear further word of this Shem that Lynna had mentioned.

"My daughter," the old man said, "told me you saved her life out there."

"It seems as if I did," Parric said carefully.

"I said nothing because I didn't want to upset her mother." He ghosted a smile. "She does get upset, you know. And when she gets that way, even I can't handle her until she decides to cool down. She doesn't trust you."

Parric laughed in spite of himself. "So I gathered. I hope she doesn't think I extracted the hero's due from your daughter after the rescue."

"Probably. She's that way. Possessive to a degree I never thought was possible in a human being." A sigh of admission, then. "A lot like me in that, I suppose. She has her daughter, and I have Redlin. We're both trying to keep them from too much, too fast."

They began walking, and the street lamps glowed suddenly, creating more shadows and pulling a black ceiling over the houses.

"Is that what you told my father?"

Wister nodded. "Partly. I tried to tell him that Philayork would do him no good. It is an evil place, you know. It sows seeds of discontent. Like an ounce of gold. You find one and you can't help looking around for more. The city gives you a sense of power, and you don't want to give it up. He was killed by the men who were cursed by it." He grabbed Parric's arm, then, and leaned against him heavily. "I would try to tell you the same thing, to give you a warning not to go there. You'll perhaps find the men who did the deed, and perhaps again you'll kill them. And then what will you have accomplished? A killing or three, and nothing more. Meanwhile, you're in that system of hell, trapped and unable to find your way out again. It'll get you like it got them."

The park was silent, lighted by globes suspended from the thickest limbs of the tallest trees. A young couple passed them, recognized Wister and called him by name. He stopped, signaled Parric to wait, and took them aside. Parric rubbed his chest slowly. It was a dream, this Redlin town, a dream hiding within a nightmare. A child could be born here, grow and die and never once know there was a green and spreading graveyard on the other side of the hills. He had seen no churches, but suspected what religion there was was based upon the sanctity of Redlin and the destruction, however invisible, that Philayork represented. He looked up to the branches and whistled silently until Wister rejoined him.

"They want to be married," he explained. "That means another celebration. They get wearying sometimes, but they're worth it. Each marriage means another child for the town."

Parric said nothing. For the town. Not for mankind. There had been a celebration the night before Dorin had left. Had that too been in honor of a marriage? Had Dorin said something damning where Orion had been silent? There seemed to be no other reason why the elder Parric might have angered Wister. It wasn't difficult to imagine his father pushing for the good of the race rather than the good of Redlin, emphasizing the values of procreation to provide generations that would work on the foundations left them after the Wind. There was no fear that civilization might devolve into prehistory, there had been too much preceding, and too much remained in the artifacts of the aftermath. Dorin would admit to some slippage as being inevitable, but only for a short while. Wister would admit the same, but not the return; what he had in this valley was a kingdom, and no king gladly gives up his throne for the betterment of the race. That kind of thinking belonged to wishes and stories.

They reentered the building through a back entrance that brought them to the first large room of Wister's quarters. The comunit was dark, the youngsters gone, and Wister hurried into the corner room, asking Parric if he'd like one last ale before retiring, not waiting for an answer before jabbing at a stub in the arm of his chair. The girl Parric had noticed at dinner almost immediately carried in two crystal glasses, tall and thin and brimming with the pungent dark liquid. Again he tried a smile, and again he was rebuffed. Wister waited until the door to the scullery had closed before laughing.

"You'll never get a response out of that one, Orion. I may call you Orion, mayn't I?"

"Be my guest. I'm stuck with it, and since I never use it, you might as well. And what about the girl?"

"She was picked up in . . . on a trip. Starving on the

49

roadside." Wister tugged at his tunic and an invisible seam split it down the center. The pale chest thus exposed was carelessly sagging, a pitiful remnant of what had been a man who must have been well muscled and strong in his youth. "She says little, and when she does she sounds like the slut she appears to be. I think she never knew her parents. Someone's castoff. I don't know. She's handy, and she can take care of Lynna when no one else can."

Parric stared at the door. "Lynna," he said, abruptly changing the subject. "She expected to be scolded quite badly when I brought her back." He looked at Wister. "Why wasn't she?"

"You're awfully blunt for a guest, Orion."

"Confused, I think would be a better word. I mean, here were three people being chased by some rather unpleasant soldier types. One is killed. Lynna gets hysterical. Another—she says it was her husband—was killed by a Rogue. I bring her back, and frankly, I'm wondering why the hell no one has even said thanks very much, Mr. Parric, for saying my daughter's life. Unless, of course, her life was never in danger in the first place."

Wister thumbed the stub again and the girl retrieved his empty glass. She looked at Parric who shook his head, and smiled again. She left, this time without the glare.

"Well," Wister said, "I'm tired, even if you are not. It must be wonderful to be young. Would you mind if I didn't answer you until the morning?"

Parric sensed the time for apologetic deference. "Of course not. And I don't really expect an answer, either. I was just curious. I'm a guest in your house, and a damned grateful one at that. I think, despite what you see before you, I'm ready for at least twenty-four hours of nonstop snoring."

Wister smiled. Lips, only.

IV

THERE WERE DREAMS: of a single eye, a single lip, floating against a background of gold—the eye winked, the lip sneered, pouted, swallowed the eye and laughed itself to banishment; of a dagger, a heart floating against a background of red—the dagger slashed, the heart parried, pulsed, engulfed the dagger and shattered itself to banishment; of a man, a tall man, run-drifting through a field of black while a winged club darted about his head, dipped and struck bluntly at his spine, stiffening it, splintering it, halving the man and halving him again until there were dozens of men run-drifting through a field of black, each with his pursuer, each being stiffened, splintered, each run-drifting slowly through a field of black—slowly—painlessly—and in each of their hands an eye, a lip, a dagger, a heart.

There were dreams: of a woman whose name was Judith with a hand at her throat and a pleading scream that covered her face like a bloodied veil; of a woman whose name was Judith with a tear in her eye that drowned a world festering with muddied sores; of a woman whose name was Judith with two children clinging to her legs—one with a coin he was offering to the other, and the other with a fist he was offering to the first.

A soundless voice commanded *Stop!* and so the dreams did, frozen in goldredblack while the sleeper shuffled a pair of dice and turned up dead.

There was sleep.

When Parric awoke, he was lying on the floor, naked beneath a worn sheet of rough cloth he knew had come from a hand-riven loom. Motes of black shifted as his eyes took in his chamber, and he rubbed them hard until his vision cleared. There were no windows in the rockhewn walls tinted a soft brown, so he had no indication of the time he had spent battling his nightmares; yet he was refreshed, and more so since he'd abandoned the soft-mattressed bed he'd been given for his rest—it had persuaded his spine to give in unaccustomed places, and after the ten thousandth thrashing, he'd grabbed the two thick pillows and the sheeting and stretched out on the pale yellow carpet. Now his back was threatening to ache again, and he sat up, scratching head, neck, beard, groin, while he cleared his throat of evening phlegm. And saw that other than the bed there was nothing in the chamber but a low plain table and a chair with a laddered back. No decorations and no comunit screen, a single bar of softened light over each of two dull alloy doors. When he opened the narrower one, he found a niche for his bowels and an alcove for his dirt; and as he turned and stretched in front of the dryair nozzles, he whistled tunelessly.

Wister had led him here, and all the old man had said as the door closed behind him was, "I hope you're not claustrophobic."

He was belowground by at least two levels, and the arrangement answered one question he'd had: how the Redliner's family managed to live in only two large rooms.

A mirror in the lavroom stopped his whistling, tempted him to make use of the removal blade that whirred noiselessly when he pulled it apprehensively from its shelf. A study of his profiles, a sigh of partial regret, and he trimmed his beard close to the jaw, tensed as he contorted to shear his hair nearer to his shoulders. Then he examined the results and nodded. Not bad, he thought, and he laughed when he noticed the violent contrast of his tanned limbs and face, and the deepcave white of his chest and legs.

Back in the chamber he pulled on his trousers before sitting on the edge of the bed and pulling his pack between his legs. A quick check of the locks assured him of their sanctity. He opened one and dug his hand inside, groping until he smiled at the touch of the handgun. It was odd that he hadn't used it against the rampaging Rogue, but he was just as pleased that he hadn't. The simple physical act of pounding that horror into technological scrap had been a momentary act of cleansing, and he wouldn't have traded it for the best marksman Central had to offer.

As he slipped into his boots, his fingers automatically drifted to the sheaths, and his smile widened: the daggers were still there.

Yet all of it was a puzzle. Wister, he was positive without proof, was an as yet undefined antagonist, but his confidence had to be almost fanatical for him not to send an agent down during the night to rid the stranger of what weapons he had. Parric never considered that it might be an error; whatever he was and whatever he plotted, Wister was definitely not lacking in brains.

A faint chime, then, and the second light dimmed into a rhythmic pulsing.

"All right," he called out. "I'm awake."

The door slid open and a girl entered quickly. She placed on the table a tray laden with steaming plates and a mug of the dark ale. Parric watched silently as she scraped the chair into position and set out the meal in order of its proper consumption. Her lips pursed, and he could see the pink tip of her tongue as she shifted a plate here, reset the mug there. Not once did she glance at him, but her back was rigid for all the bending it did.

"Good morning," he said, trying not to laugh.

53

She turned to stare at him. She was wearing the same white smock he'd seen at their meeting, though now there were tight brown shoes covering her feet. One hand fisted at her hip as he rose and took his seat. When he lifted the mug, she retreated to stand against the far wall, her blue eyes blank and aimed at a point immediately below the ceiling.

"Are you supposed to be my personal servant?" he said, annoyance at her refusal to speak making flat the taste of the food he'd spooned hot into his mouth. "If you are, you came a little late for my shower. I've already taken it." He sniffed the air around him. "As you can probably tell." Still no reaction, and his pique shaded into concern. She maintained her sightless expression, but he could see the trembling beneath her dress. "Why don't you sit down?" and he nodded toward the bed. "I'll join you as soon as I finish here. Food first, as my dad used to say. The rest is always better when you're not in a hurry to eat before the meal gets cold."

She glared, then, and he relaxed, and indicated the bed again. "Of course, if that isn't what you're here for—"

"Bastard!"

"—then it must be that we're supposed to engage in some kind of revealing conversation so you can report back to your leader my innermost secrets."

"Plaguedamned bastard!"

"And if it's neither of those, what in Winded hell are you still doing here? You're spoiling my appetite."

In spite of the venom that darkened her face, she appeared to be confused. A hand quivered to her hair, clenched and dropped to her waist. When she moved away from the wall, her legs were hard put to carry her firmly. Parric half rose, fearing she would collapse, but a look stopped him while she folded herself onto the floor, an arm's distance from his pack.

"I . . ." and she faltered, gnawing at her lower lip.

"What is there," he asked of his fork, "about the women in this place? I've met three so far, and it seems that every one of them would like to see me get into some kind of trouble. You," and he pointed the fork at her, "don't even know me."

"You're Parric," she said, sullenly. "You brought Lynna back."

"That sounds like you wish I hadn't."

She ducked away from his look and pulled at her smock's hem until it covered her scabbed knees. "I'm to stay with you."

"All the time?" He couldn't resist the insinuation, and instantly regretted the jest when her anger whitened the knuckles where she gripped her ankles. "Okay, okay, what are you for?"

"I'm to show you," she said. Her distaste for her task was uncharitably evident.

"Show me what? The town? I saw most of it last night. Your . . . Wister took me around."

"Whatever you want."

He considered, shrugged, and finished his meal without speaking. The girl unnerved him. If she was playing a part for his benefit, she was doing a better job than he would have given her credit for; and if she geniunely despised her situation as much as she seemed to, then he couldn't understand why she hadn't been disposed of, or hadn't tried to escape and died in the attempt. It was another enigma, and too early in whatever day it was. Satisfaction at consuming something more than nutrient sticks faded, the invigorating shower lost its potency. He stared around at the wall and felt the weight of the surface closing in, down, around him. After so many weeks in the open, the sudden elimination of the mountainous horizon was disturbing. He drained his mug in three swallows, then soaked his shirt and used the dryair nozzles to fluff it. Once on, it billowed as it had when it was new, and for a

55

moment he felt the dandy and missed the opportunities Central had to allow him to live it.

The girl was patient, and when he had done, she slid his pack easily into a perslok in the wall next to the bed. He nodded his approval when she demonstrated its opening, then followed her into a softly lighted corridor shaded the same quiet brown as his chamber. They passed several other unmarked doors until they reached a stairwell burned out of the bedrock. He tried asking where staff and family slept, but she ignored his gentle interrogation, only grunting when pointing the way around corners; and when finally they arrived at ground level, she rushed him through the spacious, chromium-blinding kitchen into the parlour and left with a terse promise to return shortly.

Gone to get her instructions, he decided, and stood at the window to stare at the park. By the shadows of the trees hiding the sun, he surprised himself in estimating the time to be well into the afternoon. Under any other circumstances he would have been pleased at his host's consideration for his obvious need of a full night's sleep, but this loss of morning light weighed disturbingly suspect. It was time, he thought, to stop playing the follower and work at some instigations of his own. Otherwise he would, could be in Redlin far longer than he wanted.

He was also slightly miffed that none of the ruling family had been in the room to greet him. It was as though they were taking his staying for granted—or giving him a leash so long he would never know it was there until they jerked him up sharply at some preordained moment.

He put a finger to the window, drew it back and stared at the smudge.

It was clear, at least for the moment, that the girl wasn't going to be much of a source of information. Her corrosive bitterness seemed to prevent her communicating on any sensible level. And force, with her, would only beget force. She would not be cowered, he suspected, nor could she be threatened. As for a display of kindness—he'd seen the evening before that it would only provoke her.

He shook his head and brushed a hand over his newly trimmed, and now unfamiliar, beard.

"It becomes you."

He turned, stiffly, and saw Lynna standing in the doorway to the outer room. She was dressed as he'd seen her at dinner, and she moved across the room in perfect acceptance of the effect her illusion had on him.

"It'll do until I get to the Philayork cityplex," he said, and returned to his survey of the outside he could see.

She stood beside him, not touching, but near enough to be touched. "I was hoping you would stay for a while. My father thinks you're fascinating, you know." She looked up at him, and her smile was calculating and empty. "He wants to talk more."

"So where is he? If I'm so fascinating, why isn't he here?"

"He has a town to run, Mr. Parric. Or hadn't you noticed?"

Parric nodded deliberate disinterest, shifting his attention to a group of young boys who had entered his line of sight, midway between the communal center and the street beyond. They were dressed alike in glaring white singlets trimmed in black, and their hair had been shorn completely from skulls and faces. After a moment's mingling, they sat on the ground in a semicircle at the base of a grey-trunked tree, facing a man who leaned against the bole. He was tall, fully as tall as Parric, and broader at shoulders and chest. His faintly orange tunic and leggings strained to emphasize his apparent strength, and to be sure no one missed his point, his sleeves had been cropped short to expose the tanned bulk of his arms. He was talking, and the boys were listening, nodding at intervals, laughing and poking at each other when the big man laughed.

"Shem," Lynna said unnecessarily.

"He's a teacher?"

"He does some training with the men. But mostly it's theory."

"With all those muscles?"

She turned away and sat almost primly in her father's armchair. "Theory is all we have, Mr. Parric. We're not barbarians, you know. We may not have all the elaborate and fancy magical gadgets your home does, but we don't go around cutting off people's heads, either."

"So I gathered," he said, his eyes still on the so-called teacher. "You know, I wish I had more time here. I think I'd like to sit in on some of his classes. Maybe I could learn something about theory."

She said nothing, and he could hear her stirring on the chair's fabric. Then he realized he was waiting for the chair's quiet whir as it adjusted itself to her contours, and when he didn't hear it he was only mildly surprised. He decided it was a natural and perhaps inevitable part of what Dorin had once called the techprim whirl: the amalgamation after the Wind of what remained of technology and the partial, sporadic slide into primitivism. Solar cells and no vehicular traffic, comunit/vione links and homemade ale. It would be interesting, he decided, to see how Wister was going to fit the whirl into his plans for conquering the wilderness; assuming, he cautioned himself, that these plans in fact existed.

He turned to question Lynna about that when his girl returned and stood patiently in the center of the room. Lynna ignored her, Parric greeted her with a smile and a nod. "My guide," he said to Wister's daughter, "according to her. And where does she take me?"

"Anywhere you want," Lynna said, twisting a finger into her hair. She couldn't have appeared more bored if she tried. "She knows the valley and the village as well as anyone. I have things to do today, or I would take you myself."

Like scaring up a new husband, he thought, but didn't say it. Instead he bowed, and followed the girl out of the building and into the park. Without a probe for his curiosity, she led him immediately away from Shem and his boys, and Parric decided there would be other days.

It was warm, but pleasantly so, and he resigned himself to the second official tour without much protest. And as it had been before, no one stopped them, few turned to regard them. From tailor to tinker, the shops were neither unusual nor unexpected, the houses all of the same basic design and color. If there were any scars, a half-century of surgery had admirably removed them.

"Tell me something," he said, "I see there aren't many people out today. Don't tell me they all work around here. You must almost have two, maybe four hundred."

"Some do, some don't," she said. "The children must learn."

He kept slightly behind and to her right, his eyes continually straying from the sameness of the village to the easy motion of her hips—other than that, distractions were few, and he came upon nothing he hadn't noticed when taken along the same route by the old man. He was beginning to wonder what her purpose in guiding him was when she took him around a corner and began walking toward the lake. After less than a hundred meters, the trees forced the houses out and it was as if he was outside again. The feeling made him smile, loosened his stride, and soon he was beside her, smiling wider when she openly kept her distance.

Suddenly, a man popped out of the woods and held up his hand to stop them. Parric stiffened, but the girl only nodded and folded her arms over her stomach.

"Treehogs," she explained. "They're clearing for more places to live."

"You mean, you're actually growing here?"

She glared up at him. "We do have children. You've seen them."

59

A crackling, a rushing, and the top half of a dead elm exploded out of the woods onto the road. Immediately there were a dozen men scrambling over it, tugging, finally dragging it to one side. The alertman listened to a shouting, and beckoned them past. Parric waved his thanks, and the man grinned before vanishing again. At least, he thought, I'm not totally invisible.

"What am I going to see?"

Her head tilted slightly toward him and he thought perhaps she was going to whisper. Instead, she pointed at the lampglobes suspended in the foliage, raised her eyebrows and touched a finger to her lips. And then she smiled, breeze quick, but sufficient to prove her more attractive than the knife-edge angles her usual expression molded for her.

"I am to show you," she said in the same deadpan voice, "the water. It is where time is spent."

"What time?"

"What time there is when we are not working."

"You mean, he actually lets you have some fun around here? More and more, I'm getting overwhelmed by this man's abilities."

She frowned, and he knew the jibe was unfair as he said it. Despite the tension he'd sensed at his arrival, Redlin was admittedly not exactly the future model for despots and oppression. Colors were permitted, as was children's play and adults' laughter. Marriages, births, and no doubt beyond some limits of the community, large fields where harvests were prepared and cattle abounded. But . . . and he scowled at himself. Why in Winded hell does there always have to be that damned But? And the answer was simple. It needed no vocalization, nor further thought.

The street ended abruptly, dropping in a series of wide and worn stone steps to a narrow pebbled beach ringing the lake. The water itself seemed too perfectly set in its oval basin to be natural, and at this time of year was divided into huge islands of flowering lilypads. A stone bench had been set against the high bank on the rim of the beach, and she gestured for him to sit while she perched on a small boulder just to his left. There were other couples, no more than a handful, strolling around the perimeter, tossing pebbles into the water, stopping now and then to dip their hands into the lake. There were no children, no raucous rites of courtship, and no place that he could see where anyone might take advantage of the site and swim to escape the midsummer heat. All in all, he judged it a somber, moody place, and the mountains greening close by shattered all impressions that the world was contained within their shadows.

He stretched his legs out, scratched at his thighs and stomach. A languid branch from a young willow pressed against his back. He reached up without looking and snapped it, held a length in his hands and began to strip it idly.

"I heard you talking last night," the girl said, her harshness tempered as she cupped her chin in a palm and stared out over the motionless water. "I heard them say you were from another place."

"True," he admitted, "and going as soon as I can to still another place. But you must have heard that, too."

"He won't let you go."

The remark wasn't a revelation nor a surprise, and he said so. "Besides," he added, "I'm in no particular hurry just yet. I have a thing or two to learn before I say my fond goodbyes to your lovely Redlin."

"He won't let you go."

"You've already said that, girl. So take my word for it, if you can, that he'll probably have something to say about it, but damned little to do about it. My father had a saying: I may be dumb about some things, but I'm not stupid about much."

The disgust evident in her face made him laugh before

61

he held out his hands in apology, though he couldn't stop laughing. Seriousness did not become her once he had seen the transformation in her smile, and he was already convinced she was far younger than the age that had been etched prematurely around her dawn-blue eyes and thin-lipped mouth. And when he had calmed himself and apologized again, he asked her to tell him where she was from—since he didn't think she was a full-blown Red-liner—and why she stayed. She frowned at the water, picked up a stone to toss it, and dropped it at her feet as though the movement was too tiring.

"Why should I tell you these things?" she said.

"Why not?"

A couple, young and not seeking company, passed them and hurried up the steps.

A warning shout from the alertman, and the crippling crash of another fallen tree.

"I'm to show you the field where the boys train to stay in good health, and the fields where we grow things, and the schools and the plant. This is what I'm to do. Nothing else."

"Well, as long as we're spilling our hearts out to each other, girl, I might as well let you know that I don't care about any of that just now." And he stretched his arms high and back, yawned and slid off the bench onto the ground, shifting his buttocks until a pocket was formed. Insects flitted over the lake in a buzzing fan, and they were chased by an assortment of birds he had never seen before, larger and more aggressive than he recalled they'd been from the schooling he'd had. A cloud drifted over, and the water turned brown. "This isn't a half bad place, girl. After all the walking I've done, I'd just as soon sit around and get fat for a while. If you don't mind." He regarded her profile. "Unless it will get you into some kind of trouble with Wister, that is."

"It will," she said, and her tone added, but don't worry about it, I'm used to it.

So now I'm to be a hero, he thought. Again. Only this time the feat is to save the poor little slave girl from a fate worse than Plague. And most likely the words they'll say with tears in their eyes is that I died bravely in the attempt. Winded damnation, why the hell don't all these godlets get the hell out of my life!

"All right," he said as he cupped his hands behind his head and leaned back to look at the sky, "do you have something you're supposed to tell me?"

She didn't seem at all startled. She only nodded, her gaze still on the water. "I'm to say that they will try to kill you if you don't leave here soon." Then she turned to him and grinned. "And then, you see, you will be stopped and Wister will show all the others that you are a spy from the Outfolk trying to Plague our town."

He grinned back in thanks. "And so now you've said it. So what do I do?"

She became solemn again, and shrugged. "Do what you want."

"You don't care?"

"Why should I?" She kicked at the stones round and smooth. "Several hundreds of them to one of you. It would be better that you were an army. But you're not."

"I don't get any of this," he said, sitting up. "You tell me two things when you say you have only one. First you tell me what they want me to hear, though you don't say why they want me dead. Then you tell me it's all some deep and dark plot to take away my miserable life anyway. If you don't care, why did you bother? Why didn't you just take me where you're supposed to, tell me this thing, and let me be burned and be done with it?"

"You're going to the cityplex at Philayork."

"Sure I am. It's what I'm thinking, anyway."

"If you weren't, I'd try to help you and maybe you'd take me with you."

It was a half-hearted promise he didn't believe longer than the time it took to make it. A hint of conspiracy against conspiracy that only raised bristles of suspicion along the back of his neck. It was so damned much easier just walking along the road and looking for Rogues and the occasional stray Hunter. People wore too many costumes; he much preferred the uncomplicated plumage of the birds.

"I think I'll head back for the square," he said. He stood, dusted his trousers and reached out a hand. She ignored it, but he wouldn't pull it back. "Girl," he said, "as long as you're supposed to be my guide and secret informer, the least you can do is tell me your name. I really don't like calling you girl, and from the looks I've been getting when I do, I think if you had a knife I'd be dead every time I did."

His hand was steady, palm up, waiting.

"It's Courtney," she said, keeping her face averted as if she were ashamed. "My name is Courtney."

"Courtney," he repeated. What an elegant name to be wasted on a woman like that, he thought sadly, on a woman living with a bunch of unelegant moles. And she knows it; a notion which made his eyes momentarily blur the hatred from her lines. And the bile. And the ingrained sorrow that defied the emotional vacuum in her eyes.

"Come on, Courtney. I think I've changed my mind. I want to get my things and move my corpus out of here soon. Tonight, if I can do it."

She took his hand and held it, tightly, then pulled herself to her feet and walked away, once again the servant of her masters. He hesitated before following, then ran to catch her before she reached the stairs. But she made no move to acknowledge him, and when they had climbed to the top, he paused and turned to look back at the lake, shaking his head and thinking it was a Plaguerotted place to go when you were looking for some peace and could find only stagnant water covered with weeds. Clear water was better, he thought. At least you didn't have to strain your neck looking at the sky.

And when he turned back, he blinked stupidly as the girl suddenly shouted and pushed hard at his side. A tree, old and grey and shed of most of its leaves, was tipping slowly toward him. The workers hadn't seen him and were paying little attention to the street, and as the world became fragmented with clawing branches, he spun and leapt out and down to the beach, landing on his heels, tumbling uncontrolled to his palms. He rolled over one shoulder and landed on his back with his boots in the water. It was cooling, and painful, and the thundering descent of the tree onto the steps showered splinters of bark over his chest.

He waited, eyes closed, until the echoes of the fall had risen to the clouds. Then he pushed himself up onto his elbows and grunted at the spearpoint of agony that ripped at his left leg. He licked at his dry lips when Courtney dropped anxiously to his side, her dress smeared with mud, leaves and dead brown grass. Her face was twisted with more than simple sympathy, and he saw how she tucked her right arm close to her side.

"You okay?" he asked, and grunted again.

She fussed with his trousers, pulling them from the boot and staring at the gleaming dark stain that came red on her hands. As she stared at him and he tried not to hide behind the black veil that distorted his vision, several men in varying postures of concern hovered around him. Their apologies were annoying, their queries grating, and he brushed them all off with a blunt, "Don't worry about it, just send someone for a kit."

Courtney stood, then, and pushed them all back with her good hand, snapping orders to have the dead tree taken

65

immediately from the steps before Wister arrived. They obeyed at once, and when they'd left, she traced the line of his pain from calf to ankle and slowly shook her head.

"Don't say it," Parric said. "You'd be a real lady to go with that name if you didn't say it."

She grinned, winced as she settled beside him to wait. "I'll think it, though," she said.

"Fine. Just keep it that way."

V

It was less than five minutes before a harried young man arrived with a large and bulky medikit strapped to his back. In his wake was a small crowd of the curious, though none of them ventured closer than the head of the steps and most of the men were immediately impressed into disposing of the tree and its rubble. Courtney alone remained on the narrow beach while the Diagmed unloaded his gear and prepared to slice Parric's boot from his leg.

"Hurt much?" he said, not bothering to look straight at Parric.

"Like some massive misplaced headache."

"Nothing broken, then, probably."

"Probably," Parric agreed, and when the Di's back was turned, he glanced pointedly at the girl, then to his foot. She frowned her puzzlement as she wiped his blood from her hands to her shift. Impatiently, he waved a silent signal and without hesitation she rushed to tug at the boot. He caught his breath at the explosion below his waist and fell back, his hands grabbing stones and squeezing, his eyes widening to swallow the sky. He could hear the Di protesting loudly, but the man was still too encumbered by his gear to interfere. The pain billowed, darkened Parric's vision, then ebbed somewhat when his foot was freed of its extra weight and seemed to float anchorless at the end of his leg. A face shimmered over him, focused, and the girl was standing over him, the boot clutched to her abdomen. The Di was cursing loudly.

"She . . ." and Parric swallowed. Courtney dropped the boot and ran to the edge of the water, scooped some of the liquid into her hands and carefully dripped it onto his face, smoothing it with her fingertips until the heat within retreated to sharpen the burning at his calf. A second time, and she moistened his eyelids. A third, and her hand lingered over his mouth.

"Speak of the Plague," the Di said angrily, "how the hell did you get slashed like that?"

Parric tried and failed to raise his head.

"A stone in his boot," the girl said quickly. "It must have jammed there when he jumped and fell."

"Damned sharp stone if you ask me," the Di muttered. "The skin's not ripped, it's sliced like an incision."

"Just do it, will you?" Parric snapped. "It's killing me."

Another spate of unintelligible muttering before he felt the faint chill of a numsock slipping over his foot, and after a quick count of thirty the pain subsided to bearable pulsings. Thirty more and he was able to lift himself onto his elbows without dizziness thrusting him back. He watched as the Di slid a second covering over the first, accompanied by a short-lived sensation of needle jabbings, and finally a rigid healer with a thin metal brace up its back.

The Di tapped at the healer with his knuckles and nodded. "I wouldn't walk on this right away, by the way," he said as he set to repacking his kit. "We don't have all that much call for these things around here, and they're fairly old. I don't know how really effective the support will be."

"Don't let it bother you," Parric said glumly. "I wasn't going anywhere right away. At least the medication seems to be working."

The furrows in the young man's brow eased. "Mark one up for your side, then," he said. "Last week I had to put two socks on a guy who'd cut open his arm felling a tree. Two of them before he would stop screaming. It took a third before he could lift his arm again." He shook his head and hoisted the kit to his shoulders, nodding thanks to Courtney when she held it while he tightened the straps over his chest. "Too old. It's a Winded crime, you know. One of these days we're going to run out."

"Then why don't you make more?"

"With what? Listen, friend, I tried to tell them five days ago that if they . . ."

He stopped, straightened and took a quick step to one side. Parric saw the look on his face and wasn't surprised when Wister knelt alongside him, his bloodred clothes a startling contrast to the lakeside gloom. He examined Parric's face, then ran a hand expertly over the healer. "You," he said to Courtney, "come over here and explain this to me." His mouth had thinned to the point of vanishing, and Parric almost forced himself to admit there was actual concerned anger in the breaking of his voice.

"Hey, relax," he said, ignoring the dig of stones at his elbows. "It wasn't her fault." He tilted his head back. "Those treehogs of yours just don't know how to tell a warning is all. They must have been napping or something. She hurt her arm, too, in case you're interested."

Wister, his hand raised in a brisk summons, reached out for the girl's hand and pulled himself upright. A look turned her injured arm to him and he held it gently, prodding and watching the pain sweep like a pale tide across her face. "You'll live," he said flatly. She only nodded, snatched up Parric's boot and scuttled away out of sight. Wister turned back, and his face creased into a smile shaded with sympathy. "And you," he said. "How do you feel?"

"Right now I'm pretty much senseless. A couple of
69

socks and the healer should do me all right in a day or so, though. The Di just told me not to walk on the leg for a while. I expect it's only a jammed muscle or something."

Wister ducked his head in agreement, signaled and Parric felt hands cupped into his armpits, lifting him while two other men set a polechair behind him. As he eased himself gingerly onto the webbed seat, Wister watched the manner in which he favored his leg, and Parric couldn't help thinking of the training in wrestling he'd had back at Town Central; his tutor had demanded his eyes be constantly alert for the characteristic movements of his opponent. The old man was doing just that, but Parric's view was interrupted when the bearers heaved the thick supporting poles up to their shoulders, lifting him an unsettling meter-plus off the ground.

"I feel like an emperor or someone like that," he said, looking down on Wister who trailed alongside once the steps had been climbed. "You ought to get yourself one of these things. Save wear and tear on those legs. Of course," and he grabbed at the chair's thin arms to keep himself from pitching out of his seat, "there must be a knack to staying on one."

"You're in good spirits," Wister said without looking up.

"Why shouldn't I be? I could have been killed and I wasn't. A little gimpy leg in place of that isn't anything to cry about, don't you agree?"

Wister kept silent, and Parric decided to forgo further baiting, watching instead the backs of the lead men and wondering whether every village block had one of these portable carriers, or if a team of rescuers had been assigned to him for just such an eventuality. That his suspicions now seemed tinged with a hint of paranoia didn't bother him; he only hoped Courtney had been able to take the dagger from its sheath before anyone had a chance to examine his boot.

70

*   *   *

"Do you wish to rest?" Wister asked as Parric was lowered to the ground again. They were on the north side of the communal hall, pausing at the fringe of a seated crowd that appeared to be equally divided between the sexes, and representative of all the town's ages. A low, unpainted platform had been erected between two sapling oaks, and on it were arranged three short ebon benches. The center one was empty, those on the end already occupied by Lilly and Shem.

"Well," Parric said, "if it means being stuck inside by myself, I'd just as soon stick to the fresh air."

"Fine," the old man said, his manner uncaring. "Stay and listen, then, and see how we survive."

He left Parric leaning against the chair and made his way through the crowd to the platform. Almost everyone Parric could see was dressed for an occasion just a notch below formal despite being seated on the ground, and since he didn't trust the Di's healer, he thanked the men who'd carried him from the lake and hobbled to an elm less than five meters from where Wister was now standing. Carefully, he eased himself onto one of the old tree's exposed roots, nodding politely to the Redliners who turned to stare.

It seemed to be very much like the monthly gatherings in Town Central, he thought, with the single blatant exception of the number of leaders; at home they were the survivors of the ContiGov Cabinet, and the general public seldom attended en masse, if they bothered to attend at all. Here, however, he saw the shade of an era that had died long before the Wind had been thought possible, much less probable. First the baronial hall, and now the baronial court. For history, Grandfather? he thought, and then allowed himself a self-gratifying opinion that Wister would have to change whatever plans he had now that the stranger was still alive.

71

A man dressed in Hunter trousers and full-blown blouse such as Parric wore rose in the back of the crowd. Wister recognized him, and the man asked about the distribution of the entertainment tapes. Parric understood it to be a complaint that the programs were becoming monotonously repetitious, and were cluttering his evenings when he had better things to do. A few handclaps of agreement, and Wister nodded to Lilly who rose, tucked a gold-and-blue cape officiously behind her and explained rapidly that there were only so many tapes. Since the facilities to create them had long since gone the way of the Wind, she suggested the complainer always had the option of switching off his comunit's leisure phase until he'd forgotten its contents.

Applause, then, and a few shouts of ribald methods of passing time Lilly sanctioned with an icy smile.

A woman next—there didn't appear to be any specific order of questioning—asked deferentially the advisability of taking the youngsters out of their lessons for so long a time each week. She mentioned the training periods on several occasions, not in a pejorative sense but only concerning their allotment in the overall program. Shem, at a silent signal from the old man, rose to much applause, and Parric noticed with a grin that he'd changed into a loose-fitting shirt that camouflaged the muscles he'd been so eager to display to his charges. He replied that the current phase of training would be completed before the next harvest, and in no way did he believe—respectfully, madam—that his program interfered with the regular schooling. If there were other disagreements, however, he would take the matter into consideration with Wister and revise the schedule for the upcoming spring.

The applause faded into an amiable murmuring.

A second woman complained about the lack of solid nutrients in the groceries. Lilly answered her by stating the obvious: supply was running low and the mothers of the community would have to learn to rely more on the natural products their fields were beginning to provide.

Parric watched the faces of those sitting nearest him, but could find little in the way of rebellious dissension. The crowd didn't always like what it heard, but the people accepted it as a part of the price they paid for being alive. He only wished the whispered comments made during each question and answer could have been amplified solely for his benefit.

There was more than an hour of this general discussion and planning, while the sun multiplied the shadows of the leaves and brought with its setting the cooling of a breeze strong enough to keep most of the flying insects from annoying the meeting. Parric caught himself dozing once, and blamed it on the effects of his medication and his vacillation between satisfaction and irritation—Lynna had indeed made a fine case for the presence of a demon leader, but she must have been talking about another village. And his own impressions of the tension he'd felt were fading in the realization that much of it could very easily be attributed to his overly sensitive defense mechanisms, seeing only what he'd been prepared to see rather than what was actually before him. And in that respect, his injury could well have been nothing more, and nothing less than a result of a perfectly ordinary accident.

There was definitely no denying the evidence of his eyes: the population he was seeing was certainly not starving, nor was it in a state of ill health commensurate with a voracious dictatorship. While Redlin's leaders were not elected—he assumed—there seemed to be no one politicking to take their places.

Yet a goading remained. Lynna, and the offhand manner in which Wister had treated the girl—Courtney, he reminded himself sternly; at least give her the dignity of a name. He was unsettled and, when he sensed the meeting was about to disband, raised his hand and waved it until

73

Shem caught the movement and signaled Wister with a whisper.

Immediately, the old man stood and pointed in his direction. "We have a visitor," he said loudly, "as you have noticed, the first in many months. He has traveled a long way to come to us and, as you who are closest to him can see, he has met with an accident not usually included in Redlin's book of hospitality." There was a stirring, a craning, a muttering of laughter. "We will forgive him, then, for not rising," and instantly Parric felt as though he'd struck blindly into a vein of polished diamonds. "And with your permission, we will allow him a question."

One question, and he had several dozen. Using the cover of polite applause which gave him leave to butt in where he didn't belong, he ran through them all and chose the one he knew would meet the approval only of his suicidal brother.

"I'd like to know," he said, and stopped as Shem turned toward him, one hand cupped to his ear and the other gesturing toward the back of the crowd. Louder, Parric thought, so there'll be no missing my treason. He smiled innocently into the darkweathered face and took a deep breath. "I'd like to know why the Di who treated me so admirably had to guess whether or not his healers would work, when you could easily send someone to the Philayork cityplex and replenish your supplies. I don't mean to compalin about your hospitality," he continued into the sudden silence, "but I would think—purely as an unknowing stranger, you understand—that sooner or later, if it hasn't happened already, you're going to run into injuries and illnesses that won't be cured because of faulty medical applications." His smile, he hoped, wouldn't have sullied the soul of a baby. "Isn't this gambling somewhat with the lives of your people? Especially when the life of even a single man is so precious these days?"

He waited. Eyes steady on the platform. Seeing at the fringes of his vision a careful movement away from where he was sitting. Faces averted. Hands clenching. A mouth twisting in preparation to spit. A vein pulsed at his temple and he rubbed at his beard, slid his hand upward to cover the sign of his nervousness. Mathew, he thought while the reactions sifted, shifted, slowed time down to a season's crawl, Mathew, I think I have taken my injured leg complete with all its trimmings and shoved it whole into my stupid Winded mouth. And immediately he noticed there'd been no hesitant delay in the reaction prompted by his remarks and the snide and lilting insinuation of his tone, he knew he'd misjudged everything from the children to the complaints of the Di. He had misjudged it all by a complete half-turn.

Wister, however, remained remarkably calm. His head didn't move from its birdlike tilt, his hands were quiet in his lap. Shem was his mirror, his own hand still at his ear while amusement flirted at the corners of his mouth. Only Lilly betrayed her anger. Her blunted chin trembled, and a tic developed to pull at her cheek. Had she a weapon, Parric thought, he would never have had time to discover if the healer was strong enough yet to carry his running weight. As it was, she had to grab at the edge of her bench seat and turn away to glare at the branches laced above her.

And the crowd. Holding its breath. Straining. The colors of its clothes rippling gaily while limbs were rearranged in preparation for a pouncing.

"As a stranger, an unknowing stranger," Wister finally said when he'd allowed the moment to stretch to its limit, "you can hardly be expected to understand all that we do, much of what we say, most of how we live. For a stranger, your question may seem entirely valid. Had you lived here long, however, you would know that it speaks only out of ignorance. Had you been here since the beginning, you would know that while I am sometimes arbitrary—and

75

have been often and properly chastized for it—I have never once, and I'm not sure of the phrase, Mr. Parric, never once played with the lives of my people."

He paused, and Parric fully expected a group of acolytes to rise somewhere and intone a chant of prayerful supplication.

"It has been given to us, Mr. Parric, to keep some of the luxuries, and many of the necessities of the previous time. It has also been given to us to make the best of things that are not permanent and fall by the wayside. You speak of Philayork as if it were the key to life everlasting so many of history's philosophers have promised in one form or another. But we here in Redlin know differently. We here in Redlin, so close to that . . . place . . . know what it is and what it will do should we tamper with it."

He turned to the crowd, an apologetic smile beautifying his expression.

"Mr. Parric is from the West, a no doubt more isolated place than we here at the brunt occupy. In the West it must be far easier to speak of . . . places . . . like Philayork, or even Descago, Alronto, or a dozen others like them. They must be able to speak of them as though they were merely other valleys on the other side of other mountains. But we know better, don't we?"

Strings were pulled and heads were nodded, and the instinctive hatred that had hazed the park's air faded, and to Parric's disgust he discovered himself looked upon in varying degrees of tolerance usually reserved to the wise for the child.

"Mr. Parric," and it was Shem, still amused, his voice a deep and marked contrast to the irritation of Wister's speech. "Mr. Parric, I think you abuse us. I think we all feel terribly abused."

Parric met the stare and held it as he groped behind him for support from the tree and awkwardly hauled himself to his feet. He was granted a small moment of triumph when Shem noticed the full extent of his height and the teacher's grip on his expression faltered; a small moment only, however, swiftly locked into memory when Lilly spat something and Shem jerked away.

"If I was abusive," Parric said, more to the people looking up at him than to the platform, "I can truthfully say I apologize. You're right. I'm a stranger. You're wrong, however, about your idea of the West. When you have the time, I'll be glad to tell you about it." He permitted a flickering of pain to narrow his eyes as he took a step forward. "But right now, I have to admit that the accident has probably muddled my brains more than I imagined. The Di you so thoughtfully sent to me would most likely tell me now to get straight into bed until my leg has a chance to be strong again."

"Then by all means," Wister said, and gestured solicitously to the building behind him.

Parric nodded his gratitude, bowed apologetically to the crowd, and limped as carefully as he could along a hastily provided exit aisle without looking down, into the pity, the understanding, the condolences of his transgression.

And when he found himself alone in the deserted front hall, his rage bellowed wordlessly to the ceiling, echoing and sounding more like a tantrum than an explosion of righteousness. He set his teeth together and ground them; he lifted his fists and shook them at his eyes; his chest heaved as he sucked in air through his nostrils, and without caring what anyone would think, he hobbled to the nearest wall bench and kicked it with his good foot, bounced it off the wall and kicked it again, and again until a leg splintered, a second, and a third. He reached down and grabbed at the remains. He lifted it high over his head . . . and slowly lowered it to the floor.

Courtney had stepped out of one of the offices, had

pressed herself to the jamb with one hand at her breast. When he saw her, and saw himself through her startled eyes, he couldn't help but feel more than slightly stupid.

She made him stretch out on his bed while she closed the chamber door and set on the table the tray she'd fetched from the kitchen.

"I'm not hungry," he said, the taste of his error bitter in his mouth. And it's as much her fault as mine, he thought. Those woebegone expressions, the way her lips became tight whenever she spoke of Wister and her position with him. She had colored his judgment as much as anyone, and it was so wrong as to be laughable—and would have been had he not kept Dorin's face before him to preserve his sanity.

"Eat anyway," she said, "or you'll never get better."

"Better for what? For freeing this town? The Plague on all of them, damnit! They don't want to be saved."

"Who said they did?"

He stared at her, and slowly shook his head. It was his grandfather again, intruding his damned ideas where they weren't wanted. Save Mankind. Save them? Winded damnation, they were alive, and wasn't that all that counted in the long run? Keep them alive until that cursed starship blundered back through the Universe?

"Go away," he said when she began hovering around the bed.

"I'm supposed to stay with you. And you didn't even ask about my arm."

"It isn't cut off, so it must be all right. Go away. Go sit in the hall for all I care. Just . . ." and he was tired. "Just go away."

He closed his eyes and turned his head to the wall. He heard her shuffle across the floor, heard the door's faint hiss as it slid to and permitted her to leave. When he opened his eyes again, he was alone.

The room without windows had become a cell.

He knew it was of his own making. Some inner punishment for the fool he'd made of himself in thinking his was the lot to play the white knight. Some knight, he thought. With damned rusted armour.

But there was a trace of salvation that prevented him from plunging too far into scornful self-pity: his leg. Despite his earlier temptation, it was still entirely possible that an attempt had been made on his life. To drive off the images of faces raised in condescending sorrow, he conjured the scene of the accident, watching himself and the girl as they walked toward the steps, up the steps, the slow motion fall of the dead tree, and the leap that resulted in his injury. He frowned. There was something missing. He replayed it again as he stared at the ceiling. The pause at the top of the steps, the girl's shout, the shove apparently without concern for herself . . . no, that wasn't it. Back once more to the foot of the steps. Slower. The top of the steps—and he had it.

When they'd reached the top of the steps, the alertman had not been there.

Coincidence. A break, perhaps, without telling the hogs. Walking into the woods to attend to—he shook his head, ignoring a headache's warning dizziness. With life at such a premium, no sane alertman would dare leave while the work continued. And they were still at their work because he vaguely remembered seeing them scurrying about the lot they were clearing.

So.

He allowed himself a smile and pushed himself upright to look at the Di's work on his leg. Then he shifted his legs off the bed, gripping the mattress until his head stopped playing at spinning. Not that he didn't trust the young Di, he told himself, but he reached down to check the healer, pressing at its firmness until he was satisfied that this at least was not a ruse. He looked up, over to the table and the tray of food. His smile increased as his appetite returned, and he hopped on his good foot to the chair, settled himself and ate.

And while eating, wondered.

And in wondering, became angered again.

If Wister was not the heavy-handed dictator he'd been led to believe, and assuming Parric hadn't been the sole audience to a well-orchestrated charade complete with comic relief, it puzzled him why the old man would bother trying to get rid of him. On the face of it, it made no sense. But if it were true, then sense had to be found, it had to lay somewhere beneath the surface of Redlin's tranquility. The injury, then, while frustrating was also fortunate in that it gave him the excuse to remain an extra day or two, time enough to do some probing.

He leaned back and looked sadly at his empty plate. Whatever he'd been given had only made him hungrier. He considered sneaking up to the kitchen for something else, was out of the chair to do so when the light bar dimmed, the door opened, and Lynna rushed in. Her face was drawn, her hair in disarray. She was perspiring heavily, and her bright ocher shift clung damply to her skin.

"I just heard . . ." she started, then closed her mouth and stared at him.

"What's the matter?" he said. "Don't I look dead enough for you?"

"But they said a tree fell on you."

He laughed and lifted his leg to the table for her to see. "Never touched me. I got this falling away from it."

She sat on the bed and pushed herself back to lean against the wall. The dress rode up her thighs, and he decided it would be a studied insult if he chose to ignore the view. And when she met his frank stare with one of her own, he blinked.

"The girl," she said. "You treated her rather badly."

80

He shrugged. "If I did, I'm sorry, but I don't think I was all that bad."

"She said you sent her away."

"So? I was tired. This legs hurts in spite of your Di's magical powers. Besides, I didn't think you cared all that much about her. She's only a servant, you know. Picked up on the road, I think your father said."

Abruptly, Lynna seemed to remember her position. She sat up and fussed at her hair, pulling it over one shoulder and fanning it across her breasts. A fingernail to the seam in the center of her garment, and she opened it enough to allow her hand to rub thoughtfully at the front of her neck. Slowly. While the opening split even further.

"I commend you," he said, and she stopped suddenly, suspicion shading her sun-darkened face. "I mean, it was only a few hours ago that you lost your husband. Your self-control, if I may be permitted to say so, is remarkable. In this day and age, I would have thought you'd be inconsolable."

"He was a Winded idiot of the first order," she said angrily. "He tried to get my father the wrong way. He thought he was some kind of savior to the race. A . . . a . . ."

"Knight?"

"I don't know. Maybe. But he talked too much and gave these fools too much time to think. By the time he had a chance to do something, it was too late."

"Too late for what?" Parric said quietly.

"To kill Wister," she said, as though the answer should have been obvious enough to decipher without her direct statement.

"You hate your father, then, I take it."

She grabbed a pillow and hugged it to her stomach, glaring over its fringe toward the door. "No, not really. I don't think of him at all when I don't have to. But when I

81

do . . . ." and she shifted her glance to him. "But when I do, I think of him as a fly trying to be a bee trying to be a bird. I thought Thomas had had what it would take to bring him back where he belonged. He didn't."

"Obviously," he said. "And just as obviously, I don't understand a Winded damn thing you are saying. If you were so damned frustrated with him, why did you run away with him? And with that friend you won't tell me about?"

She patted the space beside her on the bed. Gently, then insistently. Parric considered the alternatives, and decided he couldn't get himself into any more trouble if he tried. If Wister was indeed out to finish his breathing, he might as well make it worth his while, especially since he hadn't yet uncovered the primary reason.

Making an elaborate show of favoring his leg, he pushed off the table and limped to her side. Then he squirmed until his back was resting against the cool rock wall and he was looking at the back of her head. She was forced, to his delight, to turn to him.

"You could do it, you know."

"Do what?"

She raised a hand suddenly, as though to slap him, and he tensed, ready to take her wrsit and snap it if he had to; but a second's wavering dropped the hand into her lap and she returned to a self-conscious stroking of her hair.

I must be getting old, he thought during her silence; this game of hers should be driving me to throttle her. He scratched absently at his beard, at the top of the brace behind his leg. Perhaps it was the medication that was dampening his temper, which might not be an entirely bad thing considering the reaction she had to what bite he had left.

"You could kill him," she whispered finally. "He's trying to do the same to you, you know." She gestured vaguely toward the door. "That business was an act. For the girl in case she was listening. I don't trust her. Wister uses her too much."

He kept his comments to himself. Silence, in this instance, seemed the best course temporarily until he'd managed to figure out which way the wind was blowing, and how hard.

She turned, drawing one leg up beneath her. He could see the rise of her breasts under the brown veil of her hair, and he hoped with little conscience that the none-too-subtle moves to seduction weren't part of her act, too. If they weren't, he was going to be mad enough to make them so in spite of her.

A demure tug at her hem settled his worries.

"He thinks he's a god or something, you know, Parric. He really believes he can just wave his hand and things will happen. He talks constantly about the Plague and everyone out there listens. I think sometimes they believe that he's never going to die. But Lilly and Shem know better. They know how old he is. They know he's going to die some day, and they know they're going to have to run this place when he's gone." She looked at him for a comment, but he only stared. "Shem, he's scared about it. All those muscles and the poses and things don't make any difference. He's scared. And Lilly is, too. That's why she hates you so much and she doesn't even know you. She thinks you're going to try to do something to Wister, and then she'll have to be a goddess."

She smiled, beautifully, and Parric was inexplicably chilled. Were they outside, he would have turned immediately around and walked away, as fast as he could to rid himself of the shadow that rested like a fresh shroud somewhere inside him. He regarded that smile, and saw that it was empty.

His leg began to throb.

She moved closer and her arm rested lightly against his leg. Her free hand abandoned its caress of her hair and moved to touch the blond in his, reaching across his face so he caught a slow wafting of a fragrance of spring mint, and saw the uncannily soft sheen that gave depth to her skin. For a deadening moment he feared she was an android, a falsely sustained siren singing him to his death. But on impulse, he leaned forward and kissed the hollow at her elbow, felt the pulse against his lips. He smiled. Without showing his teeth.

And she pulled herself back until she was resting against him. Her head lay on his chest. One hand poked around his waist, the other rested on the thigh just above the healer.

"He was a Winded fool," Parric said, "for giving up something like this for a stupid, unworkable idea."

"You're right," she said. "It was stupid. He was stupid. He should have known better. He should have known. But he was too stupid, and he didn't. And that makes . . . made him a fool. Fools, Parric, don't live very long in Redlin. I know that. I know it. I've seen it happen often enough."

"And yet you want me, if I understand you correctly, to be the same kind of fool and try to kill Wister, too. I'm sorry, but that doesn't make much sense at all."

She lifted her head, twisting so that she was lying across his lap. The veil was gone. Her breasts were as tanned as her face. "But it's easy, don't you see? So easy it's unbelievable. Nobody expects it, if you can follow me, Parric. Thomas was too damned loud, too Plaguerotted noisy about what he thought should be the way Redlin should be run. Everybody knew he was going to try something when Wister refused to listen to him, to pay attention to him at all. So they were waiting when he finally came, at night."

"A shame," Parric muttered. "Who is they?"

"Shem. Lilly. A few of the men Shem trains specially when the regular sessions are over. They waited in the corridor just off the big hall, and Thomas, the damned idiot, walked right in through the front entrance with a big knife in his hand. He didn't deny what he planned to do, you know. He tried to make a speech, but they wouldn't let him. They locked him in one of these rooms down here until he could be driven." Her face relaxed suddenly, and became curiously uninvolved with her story. "It made no difference at all that I was Wister's daughter. No difference at all. I was Thomas's wife and that automatically made me guilty as well. We both had to run."

"But if you were supposed to be guilty, Lynna," Parric said in an attempt to keep her talking, "why didn't those guards kill you when you took me back to the road to the village?"

"Would you kill him for me?"

"Answer my question, Lynna, please. Just one simple answer is all I ask."

She stared at him. "Kill him for me," she said. "I was his daughter, and he made me run."

"The question. Please."

She tensed, licked at her lips nervously. Then she smiled and rested a hand against his chest, lowered it to slip it under his shirt. He thought briefly of removing the gently kneading fingers, thought of denying what would have been obvious to a stone until she complied with his request, his demand. But when her hand slipped lower, he cursed his own weakness and decided it didn't have to be right now, immediately. It could wait until later.

There was a disconcerting second when he wanted desperately to laugh, loudly and long. The two of them in an illicit tryst, each vamping the other, and neither being fool enough to believe in what they were doing. It was ludicrous, and he bit down hard on the inside of his cheeks to keep his lips from breaking into a fool's grin.

Oh damn, father, he thought, spider and fly.

And Lynna frowned slightly when he buzzed in her ear before reaching for her legs.

VI

WHEN HE AWOKE, he was naked, and his clothes had been cleaned and were on the table. The tray was gone. He sat up and was standing in a single uninterrupted motion, but the weight on his leg nearly toppled him and he had to grab for the bed to keep from falling. Half in a crouch, then, he looked around the room, laughing at his forgetfulness and wondering how long Lynna had allowed him to sleep before sneaking off to the ends of Redlin, thinking she had snared him in some sexual web of obligation.

Righting himself, he limped to the lavroom, stopped by the table when he realized the limp was more an unconscious reaction to the wearing of the healer than an actual necessity. A careful step on his full weight. Nothing. And once used to the added height the healer gave him, he found he could move quite freely, as though he was totally unencumbered. He circled the room to test himself, then hurried into the alcove where he stood with his head under the cool water and allowed the thrumming in his ears to clear his mind for better things.

A lesson, he told himself: underestimation has been your major fault. Lynna may be the most enigmatic of his women, but she was by no means the dumbest. Obligation? It couldn't be. Despite their brief acquaintance, he was positive she knew him far better than that. Just as he was unquestionably aware that whatever emotions she may have were as miniscule as the tear of a gnat. That she could be afraid he didn't doubt, but the emotions that lent themselves to nonphysical communication were as barren as was probably her womb.

The Plague be damned, he thought, there was someone else in the world now who thought he could be used. Wister was obviously of that opinion, and so was the girl. Now it was Lynna and the grip of her thighs. For her, he was sure, he was no risk-taking hero but only an animated mold of hormones ready to be manipulated whenever her eyes grew lecherous.

He opened his eyes, and the water stung. He made it colder and increased the flow. Thrumming to thunder, and his hands into fists.

What will you do now, old man, now that my father is dead?

Wait. Work. Watch myself multiply.

Wait? For what, Willard? What's left to wait for?

For you. For Mathew. Sooner or later the waiting will end.

Okay, then, wait for Mathew, damnit, and stop playing at being my shadow. I've got too much to do around here without having to watch my step so I don't trip over you every ten minutes.

In that you are right, Orion. I think I will stay by Mathew.

Fine. Beautiful. Well thought out and magnificently conceived. For all the money you cost, do you realize the lives you've cost, too?

I don't see the connection.

Oh damnit, Will, get out of my life, will you? Go play conscience or whatever it is you're doing, go play it for my brother and leave me out of it.

I will.

Fine!

Sooner than you think.

*   *   *

He stood in front of the airflow, turning slowly and allowing his skin to discard the scent of sex; lovemaking, he thought, had nothing to do with it. Not this time.

A check of his pack, and a slight frown that it still seemed to be untouched. Then a quick examination of the dagger in his right boot. The girl had not returned the one for his left, but he decided there would be plenty of time to retrieve it. He would be damned if he was going to leave it behind as a souvenir of his culpability. He'd worked too long in fashioning the pair. One year exactly. One year to the day.

Once in the hall, he considered exploring the rest of the belowground complex, then vetoed the notion when he convinced himself he still didn't know what he was looking for. He turned left instead, and followed the corridor until he arrived at the steps to the scullery. He didn't know if this was the general exit, but neither did he feel like waiting until someone showed up to direct him. An urgency made his limbs close to uncontrollable, and he had to keep moving or, he thought, he would be yanked apart and scattered to the winds.

The kitchen was deserted, as was the main living room. A brief look behind the drawn curtains showed him nightfall, though how late it was he couldn't tell. He let a hand rest against his stomach, but there was no answering hunger. Restlessness brought him to the comunit wall, and he stood helplessly in front of it while the grey screen reflected his frown. Then he began a random selection of the main channels, carefully avoiding the vione bands in case he should inadvertently link himself with someone's home and have no explanation for his intrusion.

And there was nothing. No tapes. No broadcasts from any of the long-range bands. Static in clouds of sparks. Not even a pattern to test the screen's extradimensional properties.

Reluctantly, he shut down the power and stepped back to renew his acquaintance with the room. But he saw nothing sinister that would tempt him to race back for his things and flee. Central had often displayed spying devices, yet a check of the couches, the barkeep, Wister's chair, turned up nothing that could possibly compromise his whereabouts. Nothing, he cautioned himself, that he could recognize, that is.

The first room was the same, and he hurried to the rear entrance, frustration temporarily making him wish a towering guard would spring out of the air and challenge him, threaten him, provide him with a moment of action.

But there was only the cool night air. Couples strolling through the park, singles and small groups standing beneath the floating lamps. When he passed them, scowling, they nodded their greetings and did not move to stop or detour him. He kept under the trees, shunning the streets until whatever was driving him would run out of fuel and leave him alone. He leaned against a manwide oak and watched a young girl playing an instrument that sounded to him like the cautious gentle sunrise on the first day of spring. The notes were high, soft; her lips around the wooden mouthpiece wrinkled with her exertion, but if she missed a measure or jumbled the tune, he didn't know it. There was no music in front of her, only a semicircle of youngsters apparently her own age. They were listening with closed eyes, their shoulders touching, their heads slightly bowed.

He listened, and allowed the melody to ask questions for which he had no answers, not anymore.

He walked, and as he passed, the musician glanced up at him and her lips quivered in an attempt to play and smile simultaneously. He paused at the rim of the circle, bowed just enough for her to notice, and brushed four fingers over his cheeks in a signal of enjoyment. She played on, but the careful building of tempo told him she was pleased.

Eventually, he found himself on the opposite side of the hall. Without shame, then, or fear of discovery, he peered into each window, and in several of the rooms saw meetings in progress. Some were evidently classes in handicrafts, others in repairs—he saw diagrams of comunits, sollites connections, and something that looked ominously like a projectile rifle. In another room a group of women in their twenties were struggling over problems with lightpens, in still another, men the same age were being taught the fundamentals of natural and hydroponic agriculture. All the instructors he could see were of Wister's generation, and in all the rooms was the same evidence of pupil relaxation. No pressure, then. Work, for the fun of its necessity.

By the time he'd worked his way around to the front, Parric was ready to return discouraged to what he'd come to think of as his cage. His prowling had had no less aggravating an effect then being stowed beneath the ground and being made available to Lynna for her incomprehensible conspiracies. And if anything, his feeling of alienation to the flow of the world was more acute.

He paused with one foot on the bottom step and took a last look at the evening, the houses, the road on which he'd entered the village and first met Wister. He frowned. Wister. While it was possible that he'd missed him, he realized that he had not seen either Wister, his family, or even Shem. The frown moved down into a smile. And what, he wondered, does Redlin's leading family do with its summer nights?

He took to the streets he'd been avoiding, peering in all the shop windows for signs of activity, and found none.

He scanned the houses beneath the spreading trees for traces of meetings clandestine or overt, and found none.

He walked past the road that slipped down to the lake, but there were no lights or murmurings in that direction to tempt him off his course.

91

So he walked. Listening to his weighted foot thud leadenly against the tarmac. A breeze lifted the white underside of leaves to the streetlamps, giving them a spectral impermanence that made his shoulders hunch. He caught the crest of muffled laughter from one lighted home, from another the high-pitched scale of fiercely gay music. Silence here, darkness there. A man and a woman sitting on their tiny porch, the man waving as Parric strolled by, the woman only nodding, watching, then leaning on the man's shoulder and whispering into his ear. The sound of lowing made less distant as the wind increased. Silence, and darkness.

The houses stopped, the road continued. A wrenchingly careful avoidance of glimpses of the sky. The trees assisted, mushroom shadows that spawned wind from breeze and pushed his hair against the back of his neck, like crawling things searching for his spine. A dampness slicked his cheeks—a scent of rain to come before the sun returned.

The road grew uneven and he jumped to prevent stumbling over a large crack in its surface. He slowed. Listening became selective, winnowing through the nightsounds for that which shouldn't have been. It was a sense more than a proof, and he made no motion of surprise when the trees fell back and he was facing a broad and black field.

There was intermittent moonlight, and in its silvered winking he was able to discern arrangements of machinery drawing away in ordered rows from where he stood. Closer, more by feel than sight, and they were equipment stands for exercise and gymnast practice.

On the far side of the field, a hut and a light.

Without turning his head from the traveling direction his eyes had picked out for him, he reached down and unsheathed his dagger, pricking its tip lightly against the ball of his thumb. Satisfied, he stepped off the road, and a flurry of winged insects momentarily blinded him until his arms beat them away, up, and into the sudden whirling cloud of bats that swept out of the forest and were gone. He had no need to kneel and check to know that here the grass and weeds had been worn to the earth, and there were indented paths between the equipment he passed without examining. A stumble, a righting. His eyes, while guiding, refrained from a direct stare at the growing light to keep his nightvision intact.

Three-quarters of the way, and he heard subdued voices. Slowly, now, and in a crouch, he used the equipment to absorb his own, moon-created shadow.

The hut had been crudely made, and he guessed it was used mainly for storage. It was less than four meters square with a flat wooden roof, one window to a side, and a single hinged door facing away from the village. There was no guard posted, and for the first time he was thankful for Wister's arrogant confidence in his visitor's impotence. It was about time, he thought, that something broke safely in his direction.

Pressing cautiously against the thin wall, he eased himself around to the door, darted past it and searched until he was able to locate a chink in the studs that, while barring sight, enabled him to eavesdrop on most of what was happening inside. Immediately, he recognized the old man's nasal whine rising and falling monotonously, in apparent bored counterpoint to Shem's insistent drone. He kept his back to the wall, his dagger hand up and tucked close to his waist. Then he turned his head until his ear touched wood, and his eyes, though lifted, he kept blind to the stars.

"So? We'll do it again. I don't see why we can't."

"Twice in a single week is why we can't. You don't seem to understand the value of patience, do you? None of you do. None of you want to."

"You must be getting old, Mr. Wister. And you're

93

right. I don't understand. If I was your age, I'd be like a man full of bugs biting at my skin. I'd want to move and now to get them off before they ate me up."

A rustling, someone walking, pacing the width of the hut. The argument apparently not unfamiliar. Parric momentarily tuned out their voices as he watched a grey-edged cloud lick at the rim of the moon. Behind it, a trail of black that covered the stars.

"Then call him. What's wrong with calling him? We've done it before, haven't we? And it worked, didn't it? There'll be no blood on your hands this time, either. When he gets there it will be done, and we'll have no more trouble with his Plagueborn questions."

"Until it happens again."

A laugh, low and delightedly insinuating.

"Ah, so the insects do bite, don't they?"

"They do. I admit it if it'll make you happy. And I don't want to call exactly because of last time. It almost didn't work. And Baron's getting too big for what he thinks he knows. He doesn't even answer when I want to talk things over with him. Always someone else. Always someone else saying he's not around. That Yasher creature telling me all the time he'll pass him the word. I don't like it, and I don't want to call. I want it done sooner. I don't want him there."

"All right, then. That's all I wanted to know. You take a long time making up your mind. A long time, you know that?"

"My mind was already made up, Shem. It was the means I've had doubts about." The voice rose, then, in accusation. "And if you'd been more competent in your position, we wouldn't have had to go through all this nonsense. I don't like it. It isn't proper. It isn't careful."

"Sloppy is what you mean, Mr. Wister. Sloppy. All right, I admit to being less than perfect."

"Don't admit it, fool! Change it so no admittance is necessary. Be perfect. Be right. This time."

"Fine. Your point is taken. If not Baron, then, who? Lynna?"

"There's no time. She won't be pleased, but I have no desire to please her now. She can wait for something, someone else."

"She's going to be—"

"She will do as she is told as long as I am the one doing the telling. And I will tell her tonight there is no time left for her games. Not for this one. This one, Shem, I am honored to say, is yours from the beginning to what had better be the proper end."

A muttering. An inaudible reply.

Parric's fingers tightened around the dagger's hilt. The moon was now little more than a haze to mark the point of the sky. If he had been more sure of himself and his strength, he knew he would have broken through the fragile door and taken great pleasure in watching blood run black. But the healer and the walk had weakened him more than he'd anticipated. His lips moved to curse the loss, then he pushed away from the hut and made his way back across the field.

Rage. Like a tempest in a valley, roaring from one slope to another, seeking an exit to the clouds that mock it. It shortened his breathing, made stiff his arms and legs. Became an electric charge that jerked his head and distended the muscles of his neck. Deafened him. Tripped him, and in falling plunged the dagger into the earth. On his knees, then, he stabbed; and in stabbing, saw the solemn faces of Wister and Lilly and Shem and Lynna ripple as though suspended under the surface of a black water stream.

A new name. Yasher. It meant nothing to him.

A second new name. Baron. Yet, not so new. He'd

heard it before. Some time before when Central technicians had taken his father's tricorder and had sifted through the static of malfunction to piece together a testament of Dorin's slow dying.

I don't want to hear it. Just take it away and leave me be.

Mathew did. He told me to say to you, goodbye.

I'm not surprised, Will. Dorin always thought that he'd finally join the Rehab teams. It's only another gamble, really. He's not doing anything he hasn't done before. He probably even took his damned dice with him to play with the animals. If he can find any.

Listen to it, Orion.

Look, will you leave me alone if I do?

I will whether you do or not. I'm going with Mathew.

Then play the damned thing.

He was mad, Orion. The tricorder wasn't functioning. Something about the placement of the heads. He tried to use it the night before—

Play it!

Listen, then. I'm going now.

Wait a minute! How do you work this thing? What do you do, press this thing here and . . . I saw . . . Baron . . . and his court and will try tonight to . . . into the Hive . . . should have been told . . . when I return, I will have a word with him about this and see if there's any con . . . alive . . . across the river to . . . save . . . we should have been told . . . *it doesn't make much sense, Will.*

It does when you're there, Orion.

But what does it mean?

I've told you what I can.

Will, you've always been sly, but this little trick is not going to work. I'm not going. And Will?

Yes, Orion.
When you come back, be sure Mathew's walking.

The trees returned and he was on the street once again, staying close to the lawns, swerving only when a house light pushed out toward him. Fire had become ice as the mountains began releasing mutters of thunder. And his limbs swung freely, his nerve steadied, the bath of his fury draining to leave a residue of hatred that clouded his eyes. The impulse to murder had not been erased, but cold patience kept him from screaming.

Baron. Title or name was immediately beside the point. That there now seemed to be a definite connection between Redlin and the word, however, was something that needed amplification. Perhaps he was connected with a neighboring village, a twin of Wister's working at the same benevolent tyranny. But immediately Parric thought it, he dismissed it; it was possible, but not probable. More likely this Baron was a figure that had something to do with Philayork; and confusion again when he remembered Wister's little sermon on the subject of the cityplex.

He stopped. A deep breath. A caution to bide. He was being hunted, but Wister's own restraints would keep him reasonably safe for a time. "Twice in one week" was obviously a reference to Thomas's death, and Wister wouldn't want his children too stirred up so soon after that summary execution. The incident with the tree, then, had not been a serious attempt on his life—a delaying tactic, only, to cripple him until the spit could be made ready for the fire.

He paused upon reaching the square, searching for the girl with the music, but there was no one at all under the trees, no one on the streets. Thunder, and the instant blue sun of lightning. The wind paused with him, then pushed steadily past him toward the field. The dampness became a spattering of rain, and he ducked into the park to stand under a thick pine bough, watching the lights streak as the storm finally broke.

Suddenly, his back was soaked and his shirt clung coldly to his skin. From above, then, it was as if a bucket had been upturned, and he was drenched, laughing, goading the skies to seek him out and burn him where he stood.

"Parric!"

He spun around, his forgotten dagger up and ready, his free hand braced on the trunk of the tree. A figure in white was racing from the communal hall, hands laced over its head in a futile attempt to ward off the rain. A floating lamp bobbed with the wind, hovering uncertainly as the figure passed under it, and he relaxed and waited until Courtney reached him and engulfed him in a hug that knocked the air from his lungs.

"Hey, come on," he said, his prior anger at her cancelled by the obvious terror prompted by the storm. "Come on, girl, come on. It's only rain."

She shook her head violently and pressed closer, forcing him to seek a thicker, more protective shelter.

Thunder and lightning simultaneously. A sparkling flash, and the stench of ozone and burning bark.

She screamed and covered her face, tried to gather his shirt around her head. He looked around to see if anyone was watching, then clumsily stroked at her back and wiped the water from her hair. Of all the reactions he might have expected this woman to have, this, he thought, was beyond a doubt one he would have shoved without thinking into the farthest realms of fantasy.

And still the thunder exploded above them, making gaping teeth of the mountains, speech impossible until he lowered his head and shouted into her ear. "Girl, what's the matter with you?"

She shook her head again, resisting stiffly when he cupped his hands to her cheeks and forced her face to lift to his. "The rain," she said, trembling. "You can't stay out here. The rain will kill you!"

When he asked her to repeat, she did, her anger at his disbelief tipping her to the edge of hysteria. He started a disclaimer, then waved it aside to keep her from breaking completely. She shouted again, and he wrapped an arm around her shoulders, and they ran as fast as his leg would permit back to the hall, through the rear door and into the scullery where they stood, dripping and shivering in the center of the floor. He began laughing, quietly, at the picture they presented, but stifled his mirth when he realized she could not join him. A quick search failed to uncover something with which they could dry off, so he pushed her protesting belowground to his chamber where he guided her into the lavroom and activated the dryair.

"Now," he said while she rubbed warmth into her arms and stomach, "what's all this about the rain, girl?"

"The Plague," she stammered. "It comes—"

"You're not serious," he said, stripping off his shirt and staring at her. "The Plague was over almost a century ago. There's nothing left of it. Nothing at all."

"Wister," she began, and he stopped her with a tired wave.

"Don't bother with the details. I'm just surprised that you believe it. You don't seem the type."

"But it's true, Parric!" Without waiting for her shift to come completely dry, she pushed past him into the chamber and brushed at her hair to find a semblance of order. "We've all seen the maps on the comunit. The storms come from around the world. Like the Plague did. He says, even Shem says, there's always a good chance that they'll bring some with them. You've got to be careful. It comes down with the rain, in a storm like this."

Parric dragged the chair beside the bed, pointed for her to sit—which she did after a moment, her hands nervously plucking at her unflattering garment. He sat in front of her, his forearms resting on his knees. "Listen," he said, and stopped and rubbed at his chest. "Listen, girl, have you ever seen anyone die because of the rain? Where do you get your drinking water from? Your bathing water? What about all those crops, and that herd I caught a sound of tonight?"

"Oh, I know all that," she said, annoyed that he thought her a complete fool. "But the water is processed, as if you didn't know, and the crops cleanse themselves. And no, I've never seen anyone die because they were out in a rain, but—"

"Yeah, I know," he said. "But there's always a first time. Well, listen again, girl. The Plague is over. According to Central's records, the records the ContiGov kept, it didn't last much longer than it took the wind to pass. There is nothing left in the air, nothing left . . . anywhere. And, damnit, no one left to make it anymore."

He waited. She calmed, her breathing easing to normal. Then she nodded.

"I know all that," she said.

"What?"

"I said, I know that, Parric."

"Well, then . . ."

The smugness that had replaced her fear vanished abruptly, and the little girl pursued by demons returned. "I know that because I've been around places. But what you don't understand, Parric, is what it's like to live in this place. I've only been here five years, maybe six, but you don't know, you can't know what it is Shem and the others teach these people every day, all day, all of their lives. You can't help but have some of it sink in after a while. You think . . ." She pushed the chair back and walked slowly to the table, toying with imaginary dust on its top. "It's automatic when the heavy rains come. I didn't think

100

it would bother me. I always laughed at it. I do that a lot, you know. But I do get nervous, too, once in a while. But I was looking outside and I saw you not even trying to get in out of the storm, you were laughing, and . . ." She shrugged. "I don't know. It just happened."

"I'm flattered," he said softly.

"Don't be. It was only a reaction."

"Conditioning is what they call it," he said.

"I don't know about those things," she said. "I just know what happened."

A silence that began with clumsy attempts at unconcerned avoidance. He, turning to dislodge his pack from the perslock slot, rummaging after nothing inside; she, pulling at the table as though trying to line it up with some invisible mark. He, suddenly dropping the pack to the carpet, lifting a foot to push him sitting against the wall; she, yanking at her hair, holding one hand flat to her waist, then moving to the chair and watching him.

"Courtney," he said, "where do you come from?"

The only light came from the bars over the chamber's two doors. Her face was in shadow, her head silhouetted as it bowed and she contemplated her hands wrestling in her lap.

"I was running," she said. "Wister found me and brought me here. I wasn't from the town so he said I have no rights, but I could live in the hall and take care of Lynna when she wanted it." She looked up. "She's mad, you know, if you haven't guessed that already. Wister lets her do what she wants, but she's supposed to find people. And when she does and Wister believes her, they're . . ."

The word was damnable and, though she couldn't say it, there was no need. Parric refrained comment, thinking caution into his silent acceptance of what she was saying. He'd been done several times since Redlin interrupted him, but there was a seed beneath the harshness of the girl's features, a seed that he knew wouldn't take much to flower trust. At least, of those he'd seen and spoken to since his arrival, Courtney didn't seem determined to unleash his blood. For the time being, then, sufficient reason to believe. For the time being.

VII

WITH NEITHER SUN nor moon, nor the marking of the passage of the storm, Parric could not measure the time she took in her telling. He only studied, weighed, and finally saw in her a disturbingly unpleasant ghost of himself.

"I was running," she said. "I was in Philayork. There's a man there, in the place over the river. He has people who listen to him like Shem and the others listen to Wister. They never leave. They stay in the buildings and he feeds them. He says he has the keys to the city and they . . . we believed him. I think he was my father. I don't know. He chose my name. He was father to many, and many of the men were fathers to many others. There were just a lot of children. Not like here. No units of people. We were all people together. Sometimes rats would come from other parts of the city and the men would kill them because he said they were dangerous and we couldn't let them be with us."

Her words came sporadically, the phrases, the sentences pumped like water from a well near dry. But he was patient, and when she glanced up at him, he would smile, nod, keep his right hand to his bed, his left atop a drawn-up knee.

"Rats," he said into her pause. "You mean . . ." and he held his hands apart to indicate a rodent's size.

She shook her head. "No. People. Men. Sometimes, but not often, with women. The men were the rats. He had them all . . . you know."

"Killed. Murdered," he said flatly, and didn't wince at the glare she gave him. "Why?"

"Why not? Why not the women? Because he needed them, he needed all the women. They had to give themselves to him and the others who lived with us. They had to bring children. It's what he wanted. Lots of children, as many as he could get. He said we would become the city in time and all the lights would go on because he and the women would bring them all children."

"They," Parric said. "Don't you mean we?"

She placed three fingers to her forehead and rubbed. "They. When he said I was old enough, I was supposed to have the children, too. I don't know why . . . but I couldn't. Then, after he made sure everyone knew I couldn't, ever, he said I couldn't eat because I had to share what I had with the children the others were having. I couldn't eat and I couldn't eat and then one day he said I had to give my life for the children, and he had two men take me to the place for the walking and they were going to give me to the river. I pushed one away and kicked the other, and then I ran away."

"I'm thirsty," Parric said gently. "Would you mind stealing something from upstairs?"

Grateful for the interruption, she smiled briefly and disappeared. It was an effort, but Parric refused to do any speculating. When she returned with two large tankards, he handed her one and dragged the table over between them. She on the chair, he on the edge of the high bed.

"Is it still raining?"

She nodded, then smiled almost to herself. "If he's out there," she said, "I hope he catches it."

It wasn't particularly humorous, but he laughed, loudly, deeply, reached across the table and took her hands, kissed their palms and released them before she knew what he had done.

"You were running," he said. "Didn't they chase you? If you hadn't eaten properly, you couldn't have been terribly fast."

"I crossed the river," she said. "I stayed on the places to walk, but they wouldn't follow. I knew it. He said we would die across the river away from him. He said there was Plague in the places not made by people, and that's why we stayed. It's silly, now, but we were afraid. And so I ran."

"Even though you knew . . . you thought you would die?"

"I wanted to," she said. Her hands cupped the tankard and polished its sides endlessly. "I wanted to die because I couldn't be like the others. I couldn't give the people children and I was no good, so I wanted to die. Then I came to places where the roads moved and I went with them until they stopped. And I ran again and moved again until it was all ended and I could see the hills. When I didn't die, I was angry."

"At the people?"

"At myself. For not dying. I couldn't do anything right. I couldn't live right. I couldn't die right. So I decided to run until something got me and killed me." She sipped at the ale and looked at him. "Not even that would happen. One afternoon I came around a bend and there was Wister and Shem and some other men. They were going to kill me, at first, but then Wister decided to take me back."

"And here you are," he said, lifting his drink in a toast.

"Here I am." She answered the toast with one of her own, then disconcerted him with a look that seemed to read his mind. "What?" she said. "What do you want to know?"

"The man," he said. "What was his name?"

"Baron," she said. "Lemmy Baron."

105

"How long have you been here?"

"I said already—five, maybe six years."

"Did you see the men who came with some friends a few years back? Three? He stayed in the hall and left the next day."

"I saw him," she said. "I heard about him. He was your father."

Parric nodded, not trusting himself to say anything further until he emptied the tankard and slammed it onto the table. She didn't seem startled. She mimed him and, her story completed, the hard cast fell to her face again.

"You're going to Philayork to kill him."

He nodded once more. "But not right away. Now that I know a few things, I'm going to kill Wister first."

He expected some outburst of reaction, a shock or a smile, a nod of approval. What he didn't anticipate was her hands clasping his cheeks, her face a shadow from his as she leaned across the table. "Make me a deal," she said. When he didn't answer, she tugged sharply at his beard. "Make me a deal!" she insisted.

"What kind?" he said. "Tell me the deal first. I can't make one blind."

Her hands eased, but didn't slide from his face; her eyes looked down, but didn't stay away for long.

"A deal. If I help you kill Wister, you help me kill Lemmy Baron."

He took her wrists and pulled them to the table, gathered her hands in his own. "No," he said regretfully. "You don't understand. I have to kill them both."

Well, Mathew, it's about time you called in. They were about ready to send out an army to find out if you were still alive.

Orion, how are you?

Doing well. Keeping alive. Is Will still with you?

106

He'll be here for a while longer, I think. The people here have to get better used to him, or they'll never accept the others. It's a nice little village, Orion. You should come out for a visit.

I like it here, thank you very much. They said you wanted to talk to me. What do we have to talk about?

You're the oldest, Orion. I have to tell you first.

Don't remind me about getting old. Now, what's this thing you can't even tell our dear leaders?

There's a girl, Orion. She was part of the team. Her name's Chamra.

Nice name, Mathew, but what is this? You want my permission to be joined or something?

I don't need it, Orion. And stop being so miserable. The communication's lousy, but I can still see that sour look on your face.

It's permanent. Like our birthmark, brother.

Well, I wanted to tell you anyway. We already are joined. Shortly after we got here, in fact.

Congratulations, brother. Is that the momentous news?

No. We have a child.

A child.

Twins, actually. Both boys, and both alive and doing well. I would have brought them to the com', but it's so bad you couldn't have seen them properly anyway. They're just like Dorin, Orion. I think one is even going to have the streak. I wish you could see them.

And you—you're well? Your wife, is she well?

All of us, Orion. You're an uncle now, you know. What do you think of that?

Mathew, have you named them?

We have, Orion.

You've named one Dorin?

The eldest, by fifteen minutes. He's also the loudest. And the other?

107

Orion.
You're a bastard, Mathew.
Yes, I am. What are you going to do about it?

Courtney smiled and nodded toward their clasped hands. "Are we going to sit here like this all night?"

He started, then released his grip and sat back. "If this rain is going to keep up all night, Wister will have to stick to what he preaches and not make it back until morning, right?"

She frowned, then shrugged. "I guess so."

"Then I suggest we get some sleep. I'm no superhuman android, you know."

"What are you going to do tomorrow?"

"Don't worry about it. Something will be done."

In the dark, then, and her head resting against his chest. There'd been no gesture toward sex, only a bargain struck without words. And despite the warmth of her thin form next to his, Parric felt chilled.

Mathew, what is it now?
Have you been in touch with Will, Orion?
No.
He's packing.
Good for him.
He says you're going to need him. He says he's done with me.
What is he, a mind reader? What the hell do I need him for?
You tell me.

Dreamt.
Awoke once, straining, listening, half afraid that the darkness was not complete enough to conceal him. The girl stirred. He shifted, turned on his side and lifted a hand to shake her, awake her, tell her there was an old man

108

coming after him. His hand lowered. His eyes closed. There was no old man, he told himself; no matter what his brother said, he was alone.

He says you're going to need him.

Parric reached out to touch the wall beside him, run his palm over the smooth and cool rock.

He drifted.

He saw a shadow moving through trees, cresting a hill, fording a river/stream/creek. There was moonlight, but the shadow had no face. He shivered violently and the image wavered, was swept away by a soundless wind. There was nothing left, and Parric sweated as he groped for a denial that the shadow was wishful thinking.

He dreamt.

Awoke, and the dreams were forgotten as he tried to sit up. Fever thrust him back. His face was drenched in perspiration. The chamber seen as through pitted glass, and he rubbed at his eyes to clear them, succeeding only in aggravating his dizziness. He couldn't win. Eyes open, and the ceiling raced up toward the sky, pulling with it the gorge in his stomach; eyes closed, and a loss of equilibrium and contact with the world outside. He recalled saying something to the girl to the effect that he was no superhuman, and wondered where they had all vanished to in the rubble of history. His arms floated, legs floated, and he struggled to keep from vomiting because he knew he would never make it from the bed to the lavroom in time.

Carefully, hours long, he turned to stare at the lightbars over the doors. They pulsed, and he looked away.

He cursed. Himself, the rain, his medication for failing to keep a balance between the healing and the illness. The Di had been right; his magic was weak and growing weaker. And Parric realized he was sacrificial on his mattress, waiting only for the knife to be wielded and his blood to be spilled. He hoped they would have the decency to use his own dagger.

He dozed, and didn't want to; he was awake, and the flames behind his forehead threatened to consume his beard and turn him into a torch to light his own way to hell in the stars.

The *Alpha* drifted by, signaling its distress.

A woman came and sat on the bed. She had a broad shallow pan in her lap and from it dipped nectar that temporarily hissed the fever to embers. Her face he couldn't see, but the hands were familiar and he shrank from them, thrashing weakly and crying when she held him easily.

The Di came, and Parric grinned inanely at him, muttering and wondering why the magician was laughing. A prick in his arm, a sudden frightening numbness at the base of his left leg. He had had it amputated he was sure, but he couldn't raise his head to view the stub. The pricking spread, deadening his shoulder, his neck, spinning his head into a well where the water was cold and drowning was a relief until he was resurrected and began it all again.

A woman came, and the roughness of her palms along his side, his neck, his legs, his back. The roughness was a comfort and he wanted to reach up to her, pull her ear to his lips so he could tell her he was an uncle and of the boy who carried his name. He wanted to tell her he'd ordered a girl to be born so her courtly banner wouldn't wither with her loins. But his lips were dry, split, stinging as she placed a cup to them and slid the liquid past, just enough to prevent him from choking, not enough to keep him from gagging.

A man came and split into two who hovered uncertainly, and Parric sucked his lips between his teeth and held them while their solicitations became colors in the air, deceptively bright on a background of black. He thought, then, that he would die and not be killed, and it angered him and made him curse Dorin's name until they left, were hustled away by a woman whose hands were rough at the palms and comforting as they bathed him and dried his tears.

They came and they went and there was no time at all because the ceiling stayed the same and the bed stayed the same and the door chimed open and the door slid shut; and the smooth-handed girl once strayed to his waist and in spite of himself he rose and felt no release and felt no relief and she was gone and her laughter bright colors against a background of grey.

He closed his eyes for a moment.

He held his breath for a minute.

There were no voices. They were gone. All of them.

And he opened his mouth and there was food that stayed where it belonged. That kept his arms from floating, his legs from floating, pinned the nightmares against a background of white.

He blinked. A damp cloth washed his face. His chest. His legs. Without shame.

"What?" he said.

Courtney set the basin onto the table and pulled a stiffly comforting coverlet up to his neck. Her face was still thin and hard-edged, but the bitterness of her second skin had given way to anxiety, and in that surrender made her much younger.

"They thought you would die." She sat with the chair pulled close. Her lips quivered and she scrubbed them fiercely. "How are you feeling?"

"Like I've run up every mountain between here and Central." He licked his lips and tasted a sweetness. "But whatever was for breakfast, it was pretty good. I wish I'd been around to enjoy it."

"You did," she said. "And it was lastmeal."

He raised his eyebrows. "No. Another Winded day blown to hell. I must be turning into some kind of nightbird."

She smiled and played at adjusting the cover over his chest. "A lazy one it must be. He's been sleeping for nearly four days."

Parric lifted a hand to touch his face. Four days. No wonder they thought he was going to die.

"The Di said it was your walking, the exercise, that kept you alive. You're healthy, he said. You reacted to the drugs in the 'sock. Di said they weren't the best and you should have had a reaction sooner. You healed, but your body, he said, had to have a go at working at it itself." She frowned, then, and absently stroked at his arm. "I don't know what all that means. But he said it. I'm supposed to tell him now that you're better."

"You've been here all the time?"

"When they would let me. Most of it."

"Lynna came once, didn't she?"

She nodded, and he was pleased to see the faint star of color in her cheeks.

"I stayed in the hall. I wanted to be sure they . . .".

"Well," he said, grinning. "It's their own fault, isn't it? They told you to stay with me. Now they'll have to do the job themselves. I'll bet they're mourning already."

"How did you know? Wister is saying the Di told him it wouldn't be long because you weren't used to Redlin and it was going to kill you. It was because you were going to Philayork, he says."

A weight settled over his eyes and he closed them in agreement, opened them to find her standing a tray in her hands. She was trying not to grin.

"I bore you," she said. "You keep falling asleep."

He lifted himself to allow her to set a pillow between his back and the wall so he could eat sitting up. With the tray on his knees, he pointed to the ceiling. "What's the verdict up there now?"

"They don't know," she said quietly. "I told them you woke up and asked for something to eat, then dumped the food on the floor and fell asleep again. Shem is always there. He sits by the window and stares at me. I don't like him."

"You didn't tell them? But what about the Di? Doesn't—"

"Wister told him it was no good and to stay away. Di said he had to stay, and Wister told him it was nice he cared but you weren't going to get better and the sooner we understood that the better."

She handed him a tankard, he grabbed her wrist instead and yanked until she'd sprawled across his legs, tipping the tray and its contents onto the bed. She yelped, but he wouldn't release her. "You," he said, "are a person of rare qualities, lady." He kissed her, ignoring her dry lips and struggling. "How long can we keep this up?"

She broke away and scrambled off the bed. "I don't think I'll keep it up."

"Oh yes, you will, lady. You're a wonderful woman and you want to go to Philayork with me."

She glared, but couldn't hold it.

"You know something? Your name," he said. "It's a good one. I confess at first I didn't think it fit you. But then I didn't know you very well, did I?"

"You still don't," she snapped, stripping the coverlet from the bed and rolling it into a bundle she tucked under her arm. "Lie down and go to sleep. I'll bring something later, when they've gone to the meeting."

After she'd left, he pulled himself to the edge of the bed.

113

Sometime during the feverdreams, the Di had removed healer and 'socks, and there was little left of his injury but a vivid red slash that would scar whitely. Maneuvering slowly, he stood and braced himself against the wall, his muscles aching, his head filling as he forced his legs to carry him ten times around the chamber. Then he sat until dizziness passed, weakness ebbed. To his feet. Walking. Falling once, twice, kicking the chair out of his way to walk again. Courtney returned, and he ate hungrily. He dozed, exercised, slept.

Was awakened. He kept his eyes closed. The room was different. Light or dark, he wasn't alone, and it wasn't Courtney who was pacing almost noiselessly. There was a dry cough, and Lynna said, "Idiot!"

"Well, what do you want me to do, choke?"

Parric forced himself to relax, breathe slower, deeper.

"He doesn't look sick to me."

"It's the light. Di says it's perfectly natural for a dying man to regain some color before it's over."

"I don't like it. We ought to encourage him. He's taking too long, and if he doesn't die, Wister might not be able to pull it off."

"One more night, Shem."

A faint chime interrupted them.

"What are you doing here?"

"I'm to bring him food in case he wakes up again."

"Leave her alone, Lynna."

"I don't like her."

"So what? If she's fool enough to want to tend a dead man, let her. What do you expect from someone like her?"

A silence broken by the closing of the door. Parric sat up and saw Courtney standing in the center of the room. Her arms were rigid, her face flushed. Quickly, he took the tray from her hands and slammed it onto the table. He pulled her to sit on the bed.

114

"Do they always talk like that? Like you weren't in the room?"

She nodded, and he waited helplessly as her anger crested and control returned—a feat in which she obviously had more than her share of practice. Then he retrieved his pack from the perslock and yanked out his clothes, donned them, saving the boots for last, checking and smiling when he noticed she'd repaired the damaged sheath and returned his other dagger.

"Where's Wister?"

"I don't know. In the park, I guess. There's to be a marriage tonight. He wants a celebration."

"Okay." He straightened and looked down at her. He placed a hand on her head and forced her face up. "One way or another, I'm going to leave this place tonight. I've been put off too often, and I've let things happen instead of me doing the happening." He paused, then knelt in front of her. "Courtney, I'm going to Philayork. We made a deal. If you want to come with me, be at the lake or whatever they call that stagnant pool and wait for me." He lifted her by the elbows and guided her toward the door. "Wait. I'll be there. And be light. Don't bring the furniture."

She made no attempt to smile, nor a gesture to encourage him. She only shrugged her arms from his grip, and left.

All right, son, he told himself as he sealed the pack and adjusted it onto his back, it's time for the accounting.

Thankful he hadn't learned how to kill the chamber's indirect lighting system, he waited until by slow counting he'd estimated two hours had passed, only once allowing his mind clearance to hope he would have an opportunity to thank the Di. He knew the young man wasn't as naive as he'd pretended, and could easily have called Wister down on him two days ago. For some reason—and he didn't

115

want to know why—a side had been chosen; there'd be trouble afterward, but as slickly careful as the Di had been, Parric didn't think he'd be too severely punished.

Finally, unable to endure the sound of his heartbeat, the pulse that throbbed at his temple, Parric blew out a held breath and opened the door.

The corridor was empty. No guard for the dead man, he thought, and raced to the stairwell and up to the scullery. The lights in the kitchen's anteroom were bright, and he had to pause though he knew he was vulnerable. His ears strained for sounds; there was something, but it was too faint to be coming from Wister's topside quarters. A quick dip and his left hand held a dagger.

The front rooms were empty.

And from whatever source, the noise was louder and he decided against using the rear exit. Through the central hall, then, checking each room's door and finding them all locked. The lights were dimmed and it was as though he was fighting through a grey spotted veil.

The main door. He stood in front of it. Not a hesitation but a suspension until his nerves caught up with his ambition. Go through, he ordered. Dorin's waiting.

The street, the lamps, the houses opposite him were dark. The noise was clearer and filled the night air; and Parric had a feeling that if he stepped out of the park, the valley would be silent. He eased along the wall to the corner, pressed his face to the cool wood and looked.

A bright circle of white light from a mass of floating lamps. A crowd gathered at the rim of the circle. Within, a young man and woman stood alone. He in a shimmering blue tunic and hose, she in sunrise gold. From somewhere in the contrasting void beyond the light he heard an orchestra of instruments such as the one the girl had been playing the night he fell ill. It seemed too solemn for the occasion, a processional for a coronation rather than a melody for a joining, but he detected in its tone a restraint, a waiting for a signal to explode them into revelry.

The crowd was silent.

Blending with the wall, he moved closer, circling, and as people shifted catching glimpses of the man and woman still in their light, still unmoving, their faces down and hands clasped.

Suddenly a door opened and a red light gashed the darkness. Parric spun around; it was less than ten meters from where he stood. A pair of Hunters came through into the park and stepped to one side. The music moved into its transformation. Lilly and Wister followed, and the crowd parted eagerly to give them access. They walked in deliberate pace, not trying to keep step with the music now frantic, and discordant in its intensity. Parric moved his lips in an impotent curse; there were too many people for him to chance a rush, and he refused to free the handgun still submerged in the pack. This deed he wanted done with none of the technology of the world just past but with his own hands.

He faded back and hid behind a smooth-barked tree. He had no desire to witness the ceremony. It would be a time of sham and hypocrisy and the tattered remnants of things that had once been honorable. It would be Wister's pleasure, not those in the joining.

And as he marked the minutes, hearing the music subside and Wister's whine rise in indistinguishable speech, he wondered about Mathew and the woman he called Chamra. The younger Parric had not opted for the killer, but rather for the villages like Redlin, spreading the word as though it were a text of universal importance—he'd elected to let Philayork wait, and in so doing passed the blood to Orion's hands.

There is something decidedly unfair about all this, he thought, but he was interrupted by the crowd's sudden shouting and the dispersement of the lamps to widen the circle, admitting them all to the joining. The musicians scattered, tankards were distributed. Laughter, and ribald speculation on the man's mattress prowess. A boy and a girl raced past him, their arms locked, his tunic already half over his head as she shrieked her taunts and tripped him into a thicket.

Light for the darkness, he thought with transient sadness, and stepped away from the tree.

Wister was standing alone beneath a lamp. He lifted an imperial hand and the lamp drifted elsewhere, setting him back into shadow and turning his red garments a nearly black wine. Parric's hand steadied on the dagger's hilt and he moved closer at a strolling pace, angling away, then closer again until there was less than three meters separating them. Wister was drinking deeply from a crystal goblet, and amber liquid dribbled off his chin, spotting his tunic. He wiped his mouth with a sleeve, held out his hand and a young boy raced to him, took the empty vessel and replaced it with another. Parric thought there should have been joy in the old man's face, the pleasure of fulfillment as another of his herd went forth to multiply to increase his kingdom. But the look wasn't there. Unguarded and unaware, Wister's expression was the calculation of a general who had set an army onto a weaponless village and called it sport. What pleasure there was, then, was totally selfish; and his mass of black hair was an executioner's hood.

Parric stepped out in front of him, went unnoticed until he lifted a hand and allowed the glow of the lamps to light his blade. Wister turned slowly, arrogance in the manner in which he lifted his glass and sipped.

"I'm pleased to see you're well enough to join the celebration," he said.

Parric, angry in his admiration for the old man's composure, said nothing.

"Well enough," he said.

"A pretty weapon. Dangerous with so many people around."

Parric refused to follow his gestures. "Dangerous only for you. Fatal, in fact. I want to know why you had my father killed."

Wister paled as he lifted his glass again. "I'm not sure I accept the accusation," he said when his throat stopped working.

"As you will. There's a man named Baron, and you have a comlink with him in Philayork. You called him after my father left here, called him and told him that my father was to be killed. If it's all the same to you, I'd like to know why."

A musician strolled past, raised his eyebrows when he recognized Parric, but only greeted him with a flurry of laughing notes before pressing back into the party. Parric smiled and rubbed his free hand across his stomach. Then, before Wister could move, he closed the distance between them and guided him to a tree outside the free movement of the crowd. "Tell me," he said. "Lynna said you had plans. What plans, Wister, that Dorin couldn't help but threaten? Was it because he was from ContiGov? Do you think we want that damned city and would take it from you?"

"All I have to do is call out," Wister said, "and you'll never get that answer."

"No," Parric said. "I have a place to go to. You, on the other hand, are going to die whether you call out or not."

Wister skated a finger around his goblet's rim. He stared at Parric, then at his people who seemed oblivious to everything but the light and the music. "They need me," he said finally. "You won't kill me because they need me, and you know it."

"Wrong," Parric said, and was pleased to see fear at last break into beads on his forehead. "Wrong, because I don't care about them, and I don't care about you."

"Then I feel sorry for you."

Suddenly Parric tore aside the cloud that had bothered him, and saw Wister from an angle no eyes could create. "You're fighting a ghost, aren't you?" he said, and his delight in Wister's squirming faded to a pity that almost lowered the hand tucked by his waist. "Dorin and me. We're ghosts, aren't we? Ghosts of something you don't want these people to know about. And you, too, Wister. You, more than anything. You're a ghost looking for form."

"I don't understand."

"A pity," he said, and lunged without warning, and was momentarily blinded when the old man flung his goblet into his face, and the crystal shattered and the amber burned. He felt the dagger pierce something soft, heard a grunt that shifted upward to a keening moan. Staggering, he wiped at his face until his vision cleared; spinning, he saw the crowd still unaware, and saw Wister sagging against the tree. There was a rent in the side of his tunic, and his mouth was gaping for strength to call for help.

As he raced out of the park into the street, he thought only that he was disappointed, because he'd wanted to straddle Wister's body and watch for himself the light fading from his Plague-scarred eyes.

A shout.

A scream.

The shout rose, was joined, was multiplied into rage, and fury into wind. Footfalls marked a general stampede, but with the lamps' light concentrated against the darkness of the town, Parric was confident he wouldn't be followed by anyone except the lucky; and as his legs remembered the rhythm of running, he looked back over his shoulder.

The park seemed caught in a celebration of another kind. The lamps darted erratically under directions from a dozen hands, and the briefly lighted figures beneath were charging shadows and trees in equal desperation.

He turned. He ran.

Behind him, a wailing. Ahead, a black wall. A corner, and he took it, one foot sliding out from under him and spilling him, scraping his hands and knees as he scrambled for his balance. The pack slid and he yanked at its straps. He slowed for several paces and replaced the dagger, allowing himself a grin when his fingers clung briefly to moistness on the blade.

A cloud had buried the moon, but he saw directly in front a dim sparkling of stars as the houses gave way to trees, and the trees to the open basin of the lake. Again he slowed, staring until his head ached and his feet sensed the end of the road. Ducking to one side, he slipped along the shoulder to the edge of the embankment, searching for the extra shadow that meant Courtney was waiting. He grabbed a handful of shrub, then, and lowered himself as silently as he could to the pebbled beach, dropped into a crouch and tossed a small stone into the water, followed by a second and a third.

He waited.

And there was nothing.

A fourth toss, and a stealthy movement off to his right. He brushed a hand in front of his face as though the gesture would part the darkness. A figure trying not to be heard moved toward him, but it kept kicking loose pebbles and would freeze several seconds before advancing again.

Parric willed it to hurry. Either he would have to kill again or not; but the more time it took, the less time he had.

Finally, when the moon broke its cover, he saw she had exchanged her white shift for something black, and she was wearing leggings and boots that laced up to her knees. He stood, whispered her name and waited until she'd run to him, hugged him, looked into his face and traced its lines with hands he forgave for their shaking. Then she pulled his head down to hers.

"I heard the shouts and thought you were caught," she whispered loudly.

"It might have been close. I don't know."

"Did you kill him?"

He grinned. "You sound as though you'd be disappointed if I had. Wanted him yourself, did you?"

"You're a Plaguething, Parric," she said. "Now what?"

He straightened and looked around them. "The road I came in on will be watched before anything. There's only one way, girl. I hope you know how to walk."

She nodded as he knew she would, and took his hand while he led her swiftly around the perimeter of the lake toward the mountains that braced it. With Wister gone, he didn't know how long effective pursuit would take in organizing, or in which direction they would concentrate their hunt. If Shem was half as smart as he seemed to be, he would know Parric would aim for Philayork; and, Parric thought, if he himself were as smart as he liked to think, he would head someplace else until he was sure they would be safe.

But you're not, are you? he told himself; neither Mathew nor Will think you are, so why should you disappoint them?

And if Will was in fact coming after him, it would be at Philayork where they would meet. Another good reason, then, why he should avoid the cityplex. Unfortunately, Will had all the time in the world to wait.

And as Dorin used to say, there isn't a cave deep enough to keep the sun from rising.

VIII

THE NIGHT WENT BADLY. Once past the lake into the forest's canopy, what little light the moon provided was too fractured to be more than confusing. Frustration and caution brewed a mild panic when they found themselves moving slower than they wanted to, faster than they knew was prudent. Several times they blundered into thickets and cursed as their hands beaded blood; more than once they misjudged a slope and spilled into depressions packed with damp leaves and crawling things that tightened their skin and clung to their clothes.

Upward, angling northward. Not knowing the distance they covered, praying they wouldn't suddenly break into the open and discover the lake tranquilly black at their feet. To prevent it, Parric climbed, pulling the girl when energy permitted, and pushing her when he felt himself flagging. And just as often it was she who led, using her arm to keep branches from slashing his face, finding the hidden boulders first and biting back grunts of pain when leg met stone. They spoke little save to gasp a position, wordlessly to sound out a change in direction. Encouragement came in the holding of hands, the quick slap on a rump, the sudden discovery of a natural path that allowed them to trot side by side before the forest resumed command and they were fighting again.

The ground leveled. Parric held onto a trunk and swallowed for air. Courtney yanked at his sleeve, and his support was gone and his arms were flailing, then hanging limply and allowing gravity to do most of the work, all of the tugging.

He dropped. Crawled up against a root jutting out of the earth. She knelt beside him but did nothing, said nothing. They spoke instead through agonizing rasps, touches, and a single soft laugh. They listened, and heard only the wind that changed the shapes of the trees and cooled to ice the dampness on their faces. Parric plucked his shirt away from his chest and shook it, trying to move the air. His pack was uncomfortable. It pulled him back until he was lying on his side, his head against his arm.

"Can we sleep?" she asked, lying beside him.

He smiled, but his lips wouldn't remain steady and his face twisted in a breathless grimace. "What . . . we have to. For a while. We'll kill ourselves. If I hit just one more Plagued tree . . ."

He felt giddy, and knew Courtney was sharing because she giggled and commented on a fall he had taken—decidedly ungraceful and not worthy of a hero, she said, and he tried to cuff her and found his arm refusing to respond. She giggled again. It was dark, and he couldn't tell if his eyes were open, hadn't known he was sleeping until an insect walked across his face and he brushed it off impatiently, sitting up to see the air tinted green around them. Courtney was curled with knees to her chest, her face and hair spotted with wet grass and dead leaves, pine needles and smudges of dirt. A moment of disorientation lulled him, called him to lie back and respect the attempts of the sun to warm him. He was down on one elbow when a bird shrieked, and he frowned, remembered, shrugged the pack into his hands and quickly assembled a firstmeal for two. Such as it was. Such as it would have to be until they reached the end.

After eating, they stood. But they didn't move.

"My legs," she said, bending to massage her thighs and calves. "I think they're going to fall off."

Parric tested the injured leg and was rewarded with the ache of a driven muscle, but nothing more. It was like the first days of his journey, when his Central-lax condition rebelled and had nearly reversed him a dozen times. A comforting memory—it revived his determination and reestablished his sights.

Then a slow scan of their position, and he shook his head.

"This won't work," he said. "I'm no Hunter. I can't find trails in woods like this."

"So?" she said. "There's always the road."

The road. The swiftest way to Philayork, the quickest way to capture. The alternative, however, was a wandering and the looming possibility of becoming lost in the absolute and letting the weather destroy them. Nothing works, he thought while she waited for him to decide. Nothing works. Just once I'd like to have something go my way.

"All right," he said reluctantly. "But when we find it, we'll have to move as fast as we can. Shem isn't going to let night stop him from hunting. His people are trained."

She seemed unconcerned, and they argued for a minute as to the direction to take, finally deciding to use the sun to point them north. If the road was as purposeful as it appeared, they were bound to come across it, hopefully before nightfall. The downward slope, then, their field of vision limited, giving Parric the impression he was back in the Redlin room where the horizon was carved from stone. He had often heard the Central Hunters and Rehab teams gabbing about the freedom beyond the Town, but all he could see was the nudge and shove of the forest as it kept them in file. A look up, and the sky was in pieces. He became nervous and took to slapping at the restraints the

125

underbrush pushed at him, kicking at fallen branches and reaching down to loosen and fling to one side the arrogant bulk of rock and rotted wood. And his anger grew while Courtney spent most of her time examining and exclaiming and holding up to his face some small treasure she'd rescued from the earth.

Grew, and subsided. Her excitement was infectious. She was hell born and Plague bred, and her blindness to the world had been cured by fear. He kept forgetting the circumstances of her living, and it wasn't long before he became sullen under his own chastisement.

Noon. The sun peaked and began its slide.

Parric wondered why mountains weren't what they seemed to be—straight up and straight down.

They forded streams, in the last of which she splashed playfully and drove off the dust of their walking. It's silly, he thought, but he nevertheless dropped his pack for the game and soon enough had her sitting in the shallow water. She tripped him into the electric cold. He rolled over and scrambled up the bank, grabbed his pack and ran while she pursued. She passed him, darted ahead and suddenly vanished with a surprised shout.

When he reached the point of her disappearance, he thrashed through heavy brush, felt his feet give way and he tumbled over rocks and exposed roots and landed in a ditch. Standing, he saw her above him. Smug. And grinning.

"You're right," she said. "You aren't much of a Hunter." And she pointed down at the road beneath her feet.

But the condition of their traveling was disturbing. Parric had hoped to be able to keep a slow running pace, but here the road had been churned into obstacles they spent more time climbing over than walking around. Paradoxically, it was also heartening. From the records and stories he'd gathered at Town Central, he understood that the outlying villages became almost nonexistent the closer one came to the Philayork cityplex. There had been no need for them, and they had vanished; no places, then, like Redlin to keep in minimum repair for their own infrequent use. There were also fewer birds, and the insects were unchecked. Defoliated trees and shrubs. Clouds of dark buzzing. Anthills that rose half a meter out of the ground. As though a wall had been breached and evolution snarled. As he helped the girl through a tangle of dead trees, he wondered how she'd managed to get this far without being eaten alive.

And always the glances behind, the straining for sounds unnatural to the forest.

He slept little that night, was irritable the next day.

He was puzzled, and the constant tuning of his senses to mark their pursuers was beginning to tire him. By all rights and imagination, Shem should have caught up with them, would have taken immediately to the road, stringing enough of Redlin's Hunters along the way to mark the places where Parric and the girl would come crashing out into the open. Yet there was nothing; no shouts, no gunfire, no tramping of Hunters' boots over the debris in the road.

It bothered him because no answers would come, and even in sunlight he hated the dark.

Dusk. There was no counting the days. Courtney was no longer able to disguise her limping. Parric, angry and fearful she had somehow managed to cripple herself, carried her off the road into a tallgrass field. The mountains had become hills and the valleys widened, crisscrossed by rivers and streams darted with fish and frequented by waterfowl. He set her down beside a broad and deep stream and unlaced her boots. Her feet were swollen, insect bites raising ugly welts and running pustules.

"I didn't want us to stop," she said without apology.

Parric had no comment. He covered her feet with balm after a washing in the water, then wrapped them lightly in a bandage of damp leaves. "We might as well stay the night," he said, reclining beside her. "It seems peaceful enough."

"It should be," she said. "I haven't seen anything but a bird in days. It's nice, though, after that place where there were none."

He stared at the land ahead of them, the suggestion of hills he estimated were a day's travel away. "All right," he said. "How long?"

She looked away, plucking grass and tossing it into the stream. "I can't be sure."

"Yes, you can," he said. "How long?"

"Over there," and she pointed to where he'd been looking. "On the other side."

Parric slid down the steep bank to the water, reached down to splash handfuls into his face. A breeze brushed his hair around into his eyes, rustled the reeds that served as a screen for nests and dens. Her reluctance, sudden and snappish, bothered him. He had thought she wanted nothing more than to witness the death and destruction of the life she'd fled from, and the man and the men who had driven her out. But during the past two days she'd become withdrawn, dragging and having to be prodded to maintain his pace. At first, he'd decided it was the fear of her returning, the spade of their approach unearthing things she would just as soon not recall outside her dreams; that was understandable, just as it was wrong. There was far more to it, an alteration he hadn't noticed until the look she gave him when he asked for the city's location. She was less bitter, less filled with hate—which had once been a good thing because he had counted on it to feed him, seeing it a complement to his own, and a rationale for his continuing. As it faded, wavered, he saw himself increasingly alone, and increasingly wondering.

"Hey," he said. "Remember that deal we made?"

"We didn't make a deal."

"Sure we did."

"No, we didn't, Orion," and the name sounded strange, the first time she'd called him anything but Parric. "You said we could make a deal, but there was none. You wanted to kill Wister and Baron, and you've done the one and I'm going to help you with the other. There wasn't a deal, though. You just said that to get me to come with you."

"Now wait a minute," he said, turning on his buttocks to look up at her, still on the top of the bank. "That's not strictly true, you know. I'm not trying to use you, if that's what you're saying."

She shook her head. "It isn't." There was a smile, but nothing inside it. "You can't use me. I'm all used up. I wanted to come, and here I am."

"Then, what's the matter, girl?"

"My name is Courtney," she said. "You told me it fit me. You said that back there. Use it, then, and don't call me girl."

He held up a palm to ward off her anger, then pulled a dagger free and dug at the ground.

"I've just been wishing we were heading back the other way," she said.

"What? What the hell for?"

"I don't know. To see that place of yours, to see the people the way they were before we were born. I don't know. I don't understand it yet. When I do, I'll let you know."

"It's not all that wonderful, you know," he said. "If I made it sound that way, I'm sorry. But it's not."

She tossed a rock over his head into the water. "That old man, the one with your father when he was here. You never talk about him. Who was he? A friend?"

Parric debated avoiding the question as he had done

when it had been asked of him earlier. But now there was no purpose.

"He was a friend, yes. A friend of my father's, and of my grandfather's."

"So old?"

"He was born old, Courtney. He's an android."

Her eyes widened so far, he couldn't help but chuckling.

"He's not a Rogue," he said. "Though sometimes he's a pain in the neck just the same. You see, the place where I live makes androids like they did before the Plague. Good ones. They help with the research, the labor, the teams we send out to bring the villages back to the government." He frowned, then, and returned slowly to the top of the bank and sat beside her. "It's funny, but there were only a couple or so that weren't infected by the Plague, and to build them now is slow business. I don't think there are more than three or four dozen all together, and there are none outside Town Central. None," he corrected quickly, "that are trustworthy."

Courtney was staring at some invisible and distant point. "That nice, cranky old man wasn't human?"

Parric laughed. "Don't ever say that to him, young lady. He thinks he's as human as anyone in the world." Then, softly: "And more human than my brother or I, I think."

She shook her head, scratched her arms vigorously. "It's a strange place you live in, Orion."

"I told you it wasn't a heaven."

"Oh, you've made that clear enough. Clear enough, though, to make me wonder a little just what a heaven is." This time the smile was shy. "It's your fault, you know."

"Winded nonsense," he muttered, and drove his blade deeply into the ground, left the hilt poking toward the sky while he stripped and waded into the stream to bathe himself. The water was cold, an awakening that evaporated the darkness he felt gathering at his eyes, and pooling inside. He turned his back to her and stared down at the swirling around his legs.

"Parric," she called out, "what are you going to do when you've killed him?"

He squatted and punched at his reflection. One thing at a time, he wanted to tell her; you can't make plans for the aftermath of a killing, not when the killing has been coming for years, not when the axis that pierces your lungs and regulates your heart has been greased by blood that's already been spilled.

"I'll think of something," was his answer, finally, and he lay down in the water and submerged his head to drown her reply and keep her from shaking him further.

And when he stood, dripping and shivering, she was standing at the bank, holding out a foodstik. Chewing. Slowly. As though there was a taste she could locate and savor.

"Courtney, I'm sorry," he said, wading toward her, reaching out and taking the food with one hand while trying to dress with the other. "It's so close to the end, I guess I'm just tired. I can imagine how you must feel."

"I don't think so," she said, and when he'd finished dressing, she sat crosslegged beside him.

The sun fed their shadows, cast them unmoving over the stream and into the rushes on the opposite bank. Birds filled the air to feed and to mate, and they watched in silent amazement as a clan of small brown creatures with fur like thin spines slipped into the water and swam past them upstream. It grew dark, but the air remained warm. He told her again of the day he'd met Lynna and Thomas and the battle with the Rogue. It hadn't meant to be a warning, but suddenly they were closer together, scanning the open field and feeling tension revive. Parric smiled to himself when he caught a vagrant thought of the club he'd left behind, and the way he'd swung like a madman until the crazed android had been battered into scrap. And back to Wister's daughter again, in a new and more frightening light: Courtney had called her mad, and he was inclined to agree—a woman who gave herself to men she knew were going to die, the men she herself had probably labeled in meetings with her father and Shem. And more horrifying, her escaping with them so she could watch them die. It wasn't hysteria at her near-capture when she'd pounded Thomas's back before Parric had intervened—she was frustrated that he hadn't been able to run any farther. A vampire, he thought, sucking at the fear she herself had created. An instant's regret, then, that she hadn't gone the way of her father.

"Parric?"

"What? I'm sorry, were you saying something? I was just doing some thinking."

"No." She was on her knees, facing the road. "I just thought I heard something out there."

Nerves, he was going to reassure her, but her hand grabbed at his arm. Those weeds in the field not flattened by a recent storm were brown and sagging of their own weight; but there was still a low barrier and he had to rise to a crouch to see what had startled her. The light had become hazy, was darkening rapidly, but not rapidly enough to prevent him from spotting three figures moving along the roadbed. By their costumes they were Hunters, and by their carefully spread arrangement and deliberate movement, they were practicing their craft. He had no doubts of their origin; he hadn't passed a village since leaving Redlin, and no Hunters' pack would stray this far from its base. Shem, then, had finally caught up with them.

"They won't see us," she whispered without much conviction.

A gesture contradicted her. They wouldn't be Hunters unless they could read, and if they could read the place

132

where he'd carried Courtney into the field, they would be on them, and soon.

"Shem?"

He shrugged, then shook his head. None were tall enough, nor broad in chest and shoulders. He put a palm to his forehead, slapped it lightly to drive off despair and make room for planning. The trio had to be merely the tip of a wedge, an advance point detailed to leave signs for those who followed. Which meant that at least twice their number were in the main party. What he couldn't understand, however, was why they weren't moving more rapidly. With the skills they were reputed to have, they would need only that single glance to read what they had to know; yet they were almost visibly holding themselves back, waving to each other, the sound of low talking drifting over the field. Perhaps it was arrogance, or a professional confidence, but Parric wasn't about to stand up and ask questions. He gestured rapidly, and Courtney brought him his pack.

The Hunters stopped and came together, stretching as though trying to see over and through the obstacle of weeds.

Parric handed the girl both his daggers. She frowned, pointed at his hands and he lifted a finger in slight reprimand. She raised an eyebrow in question, and he held up his hands to show they were empty, then reached into the pack and pulled out his handgun. She stared, and he was stopped for a long minute when he realized she didn't know what it was. Carefully, he fit its grip to his fingers and patted the triangular, downward curving guard that swept back over his wrist. He aimed at a tree, waggled his finger, then pointed at the rifles the Hunters were carrying.

They stepped off the road, separating, weapons at the ready.

Parric tugged at her hair until she set an ear against his lips. "They won't kill us now. Shem will have told them

133

to hold us until he catches up. But they're going to have to defend themselves if we get at them first." She nodded, and he felt the fear that made shallow her breathing. "I want you to lie down, here, face up. Sleep, you understand?" She nodded again and, when he released her, quickly set a kiss on his cheek. He smiled, pushed at her nose with one finger and slipped down through the reeds until his head was level with the top of the bank. It would be easy to kill them all, he thought, if his shots were true and they were too confused to react swiftly. But he couldn't take the chance, not with Courtney here. If he got only the first, the others would drop and there would be no second chance. He needed the girl. To take him to the city.

From beneath his chest he dislodged a stone and tossed it as far ahead as his awkward position would allow. He heard Courtney stir, then become quiet. And there was silence complete except for the stream that betrayed itself behind him. And footfalls. The unavoidable brush of cloth against weeds. He glanced up through the reeds and saw a head floating against the star-pocked sky. It approached and grew shoulders, and there was another off to its left, and beyond that still another. A year at a time, Parric shifted his weapon into position in front of his face. He would have to wait until they were gathered around the girl before he could do anything, and even then there was no guarantee he could act rapidly enough to protect her. It was a stupid plan, he thought. He should have surrendered them both and waited for an opportunity to escape before Shem and the others arrived; he should have fired first and thought later, trusting to his luck and the practice of his aim to dispatch the Hunters before they spotted him; he should have lain with the girl because they'll be suspicious as soon as they see she's alone with no evidence of their staying for the night.

He should have. But he didn't. And he cursed the stars for the folly of his name.

A snap, and the nearest Hunter froze, lifted the hand that held his rifle and signaled for the others to join him. He had abandoned his crouch and was walking without pretense of deception directly toward Courtney.

And Parric cursed again and closed his eyes quickly.

The middle Hunter had ignited an incandescent torch, a slim cylinder with a globe for a head that directed a sweeping shaft of whitebright light around the area as his fingers deftly positioned its three-quarter hood. The beam darted past the girl toward Parric, who tensed and raised his handgun, then darted back and steadied on her face. She stirred, fluttered her eyes and sat up with a convincing short scream.

Her hands were hidden, pressed to the ground behind her buttocks.

Instantly, the three stood in front of her, watching as she shifted nervously to squat on her haunches. The light stayed on her face, and she was disembodied, eyes nose mouth only glaring at her captors. It was no use now; his handgun was useless. Shoot one, and Courtney would die, the others would fire in the direction of his beam. It was the trouble with civilian lasers, he thought angrily—they took too long when their assembly was compressed into confinement weapons such as his; but the rifle with its heavy and massive stock was as rapidly deadly as a projectile gun.

It was up to the girl, then. She would have to provide him with the opportunity. And in thinking, he disengaged his hand and placed his palms even with his chest, his boots lifting slowly to find purchase on the bank.

"Where is he?"

Courtney shook her head. "He's dead," and jerked a shoulder back.

The Hunter carrying the light bent over to fraction the space between their faces. The other two would be involuntarily glancing at the area she'd vaguely indicated; Parric found himself thinking a short prayer.

Suddenly she moved, her hands whipping from behind her, and in the instant they were visible the twin daggers were comets flashing blue fire. They plunged into the Hunter's stomach and Courtney's momentum carried them both into a tangle. Parric, immediately he saw her tense for the leap, had sprung from the bank and was on the nearest man before he could turn, spilling him with a shoulder and jumping over the girl onto the last, who was too confused to do anything but gape.

The torch lay where it had fallen, its single narrow beam escaping upward to be swallowed by the pale rising moon.

Parric's hands had slammed into his man's chest and stomach, toppling him, and as he fell, Parric wrenched free his rifle and spun around. Courtney had already left her dead Hunter and was sprawling over the struggling, shouting form of the other. Parric moved, was beside her, had a hand to her shoulder and pulled her to her feet. "Hey, it's me!" he shouted when she punched at his face, and he flung her aside, using the rifle's butt as a club alongside the last Hunter's head.

Courtney had landed heavily, and her hand tipped the torch so a shaft poked through the reeds and illuminated a thin, transparent ribbon of wavering water.

Parric knelt and lightly placed two fingers where his blow had landed. There was blood, but the man would recover. He nodded, checked the body of the torch bearer and yanked the daggers from his stomach, tossing them behind him to clean later.

And the man he'd disarmed was on his knees, hugging his stomach and retching dryly. It was an unpleasant sound and Parric wanted him to stop it. He felt his hands tightening, searching for the depression that would activate the weapon. He had to stop it. It was disgusting. More so now, because he could hear the man crying.

Courtney came up beside him. The torch in her hand. She directed its hood so a beam fell on the Hunter.

"A boy," she said flatly. "That Plagueborn bastard is sending us boys."

Parric dropped the rifle and toppled the boy onto his back. He stripped off the trousers and tore them in half with the aid of a knife Courtney pressed into his hand. He paused, then, until he saw it had been washed by the stream; when he looked up at her, he couldn't smile his thanks.

He tied the boy's arms and legs as tightly as he could, and sat, and waited.

"So you're a Hunter," he finally said, hoping his sneer seemed more evil than he felt.

"We're not going to kill you," Courtney added, but she wasn't believed. His face was pale beneath the smears of black applied to his cheeks and forehead, over his chin. He tried to break his bonds and, in failing, tried further to look defiant.

Suddenly Parric reached out and yanked off his skull cap. "Not only a boy," he said as though describing an experiment, "but a child, as well. Look how soft the hair." And he shook his head.

"I'm not a child," the boy said.

"It talks," Parric said. "So look, not-a-child, I'll grant you that if you tell me how far ahead you were of the others."

"None," and he flinched when Courtney brought up the torch and glared it into his face.

"Come on, now, boy-man, I've given you your life. How many? Who?"

It continued for an hour, Parric easily falling into the role of persecutor while Courtney became his soft-talking friend. They badgered, confused, soothed, poked, calmed, threatened. When he started to cry, they sat back

137

and waited. He stiffened, and they began again. Parric didn't worry about the time he had—if there were many and near, it was already too late; and if they were camping, he had all night. He told himself that, but his patience wouldn't listen, and over Courtney's protests he grabbed the boy's throat and held it lightly, firmly, squeezing just enough to signal his intention.

"Tell me," he said. "After the old man died, how many men did Shem send after us?"

The boy shook his head.

"You're saying no? Do you mean he sent none, no one but you three big important Hunters?"

Courtney put a finger to his shoulder, but he ignored it. The stars glaring into his back had begun to bother him, and he wanted to be gone, into the woods across the road and to sleep, if he could, to run, if he had to.

"I'll tell you what," he said, sitting hard on the ground as if resigned by the boy's intransigence. "We can't leave you here, I guess, and she already promised we wouldn't kill you so I'll have to stick with that. It seems, then, that you have us at your mercy," and he tugged sharply on the cloth that bound him. "But we can take you with us, can't we? Tell me, boy, how would you like to go to Philayork?"

In the harsh light of the torch, the boy had lost all claim to age, and now his face broke into rivulets of perspiration that ran like tears and dripped from his chin. He looked down, gnawing at his lips, sniffling, then turning his head to wipe his cheek against his shoulder.

"Ain't dead," he muttered.

Parric grabbed his jaw and yanked his face up. "Ain't dead? Who ain't dead?"

"Wister," the boy said, finding courage in Parric's disbelieving anger. "You didn't kill him. He ain't dead."

"I saw him," Parric said, measuring his words, speaking more to himself than to the others. "Winded damn soul, I saw him fall! You can't fool me, boy Hunter, I did him myself.''

"He ain't dead," the boy insisted. "His side hurt bad. Di says he came closer than you, but he ain't dead.''

"Then he's coming," Parric said.

The boy nodded, and he was so close to gloating that Parric had to grab at the ground to keep from tearing out his throat. "Mr. Wister, four more, maybe, I don't know. Not counting me or them. Mr. Wister, he says we're not to hurry because he knows where you are. He'll come to get you out, he says. Sooner or later.''

"And the girl," Parric said, grabbing the torch from Courtney's hand and shining it at her face. "What about her? What did he say about her?''

"Nothing. We were to hold you if we found you, and wait for Mr. Wister. He didn't say nothing about her. I guess we would have done her. Mr. Wister didn't say no.''

A hand flashed, met flesh, and it was a moment before Parric realized it had been his own. He stood and pulled Courtney to his side. "I'm going to leave you here, boy Hunter. I'm sorry, but I can't take you with us. I know how bad you're going to feel.''

"I have nothing to eat." The gloating had vanished, the fear returned as Parric tucked the torch into his waistband.

"If it's only for a couple of days, boy Hunter, you won't starve. Oh, a Rogue may come about, but I doubt it. And there's not enough of you for the insects to bother with. If you get thirsty, you can crawl, somehow, to the stream over there. Maybe your friend will be able to help, but I doubt it. Just be careful you don't drown, boy Hunter. The bank is slippery.''

Quickly, then, he snatched up the three rifles and, with Courtney following, made his way back to the road, ignoring the sudden shrill shouts of the boy he'd left in the dark.

Boy. Man. They were one and the same when it came to stealing his breath. He felt as though a reprieve had been

139

given. Having killed Wister once, another chance was handed to him to relive the time and do it again. A moment of his own choosing, however, and preferably in the canyons of Philayork where Dorin had been deprived of that simple basic choice.

IX

THE DAYS TO the hills and over were two; and they were decades, centuries, a heartbeat long.

"Your beard needs trimming, Parric."

"It was long when I first came, and I think you can stand it for a little while longer."

"Is that what you tell me is a play with words?"

"A play is for actors. I do my own creating."

He discarded the rifles the first afternoon—reluctantly, but they were too heavy and he was too much hurried. He found a ravine that he fed with their stocks.

"You talk in your sleep, you know."

"Save your breath. Use it on your feet."

"Odd words. You say a lot of odd things, even when you're awake."

"What odd words?"

"Alpha, for instance. Is it a name?"

"A dead name, Courtney."

"I like it."

"Don't bother."

"Why don't you let me help you with that pack? I'm no child, you know, not like that boy back there."

"I'll carry my own weight."

141

"Are you afraid I'll steal something? Don't you trust me after all this time?"

"You're getting better, girl. You're beginning to sound like a woman."

"What is that supposed to mean?"

"It doesn't mean anything. I'm sorry."

"Then let me help you with the pack."

"No."

"Will you go back to that Town Central when you're done, Orion?"

"Probably. There's no place else I want to go."

"Why, though? All this way and then just go back? Don't you think your people might like it here?"

"I don't speak for them. They have their own minds."

"Well, good for them. I didn't think you liked them very much."

"Like has nothing to do with it."

"You were talking again last night. Who is Mathew?"

"My brother."

"Does he look like you?"

"He's shorter."

"Does he have the light in his hair?"

"More pale."

"What does he do?"

"Plays god."

"What are you going to do the first thing in the city?"

"Turn on the lights."

"That's funny. Why?"

"You know, I think you had to run away because you talk so much. Is that why? Come on, tell me the truth."

"Sure I talked a lot. There wasn't anything else to do. And you haven't answered my question."

"Which one?"

142

"About the lights."

"I don't know."

"If you knew, would you tell me?"

"You know something, girl, I really think I would. I don't know why, but I really think I would."

The land fell away and became flat, a man-inspired plain that had long ago succumbed to natural reclamation. It fell away, and Parric was faced with the cityplex ghost.

There were walls of a kind, but no parapets or turrets from which banners extended and trumpeters announced and ladies in gold waved farewell to the sun; there were doors, of a kind, but no massive gates or serpent-filled moats or bridges that denied entrance to alien foes; there were roads of a kind, but no glimmering jewels set into a path lined with the faithful stretching hands toward his hem.

And despite all his readings, studies, queries and dreams, Parric was silenced in solemn disappointment.

The road led directly toward a huge tunneled maw, double-tiered and canopied in glass. To either side were the buildings that forced him to lean backward as he searched for their varied roofs. Half their distance from the ground to the clouds they were windowless and of a sullen red stone that refused to look to the mountains of the west—for the poor and uncaring, he remembered, and wondered; and the glittering windows that appeared at irregular intervals above the blankness were for the rich and the romantic who needed glimpses of green. To the right and the left they curved without stopping, the only breaks were the tunnels that housed the links between sectors. The road divided and divided again, each arm stretching toward the transystem Walkways, and he allowed Courtney to lead him farther north. A half a day before she stopped him.

"We'd better sleep out here tonight," she said. "It gets dark fast inside."

Parric balked as he paced in front of a Walkway entrance, his hands rubbing at his thighs, beard, sides of his head. He was trading one forest for another, and he didn't like it. The first he knew well, but this . . . he would have to go one trusting her, and he didn't much care for the feeling of chains. But he agreed and handed her the gun, showed her how to use it to kindle a fire; the monolith 'plex was too high for his comfort, and he wanted something moving besides his own breathing.

Then he walked along the city's base and touched at the walls, pried at the mouths of man-high conduits that opened, after all, into a moat, a trench in which nothing grew but stubbed grey grass. The pictures he'd seen had not prepared him for the sheer mass of its appearance, and he speculated as he returned if Dorin had felt the same apprehension, the same uncertain fear that bordered on superstition.

"It's a peculiar thing," he said with the fire between them, "but whoever's left in there is afraid to come out because of what the Plague had done." He shook his head. "And out here there are people like Wister in Redlin who are afraid to go in because of what the Plague had done. It's fantastic, but you could probably wander around in there for years and never come to an end."

"The sea is the end," she said, the flames giving a color to her face that the sun had not. "Have you ever seen the ocean?"

He wanted to lie because somehow it seemed important, but knew she'd trap him before he'd finished. "No," he said. "The hills and the mountains always had enough . . . I don't know, bigness, for me."

"I'll show you, then," she said. "If you've never been frightened, it will frighten you."

"Thanks, but no," he said, smiling. "I'll wait, if you don't mind."

"Aren't you worried about Wister?"

He grabbed another handful of twigs and grass and set it carefully onto the fire. He said he wasn't; if the old man was taking his time, it meant he planned to move into the cityplex despite his own warnings. The worry was keeping the distance between them the same until he had rooted out Baron.

"Hey," she said softly, her hands stilled in the act of scattering away the evening's embers.

Parric turned sharply, straightened and became rigid. A figure plodded toward them. Quickly he scanned the plain and the wall of the forest for signs of others in pursuit. But there was no one but the single man, stooped slightly beneath a bulky pack. He heard Courtney scrambling to her feet behind him, then heard nothing but rage bellowing windlike in his ears. A drop of spittle bubbled at the corner of his mouth, his forehead tightened, and when the girl tugged at his sleeve he slapped her away. He looked down and saw a knife in his hand, glanced up at the approaching man and more in futility than anger he threw the weapon. At the cityplex wall. Saw it flash short and drop into the trench.

Skyward, then, and against the bright morning blue there was a fist clenched whitely, steadily, slowly dropping down until it rested against his thigh.

The man stopped and unslung his back. Grey hair, age imprinted artfully in his lean face and long-fingered hands, a clever hint of wattles at the throat, the nondescript clothing a half-size too large to lend fraility to the image. All of it deception, except for the eyes.

"Orion."

Parric swayed. To cry out would be too easy now, to

145

rant a waste of strength against a thing too strong. He wanted to demand that it be gone, be done with its hovering over him like that damned unseen *Alpha* that drifted mute and aloof like a god waiting for a priest. From the moment of that last talk with his brother, he'd felt Dix waiting, patiently as only an android could be; he'd felt it and brushed the feeling away because he had to be alone. But he never had been, and that was the hell of it.

"I know you."

Courtney came out from behind Parric and stood in front of the android who bowed and took her extended hand solemnly. She looked back over her shoulder and grinned. "It's the old man, Orion! You didn't tell me he was coming with us?"

"I didn't know," he lied.

Dix gestured toward the wall. "You going in there?"

Parric nodded, once. "I suppose you insist on coming along?"

Dix shrugged. "If I can help."

"Of course he can," the girl said, rushing back to the fire to gather up their belongings. "Orion, he's just what we need!"

Parric ignored her. He moved until there was an arm's length between them, then reached out to touch the old man's chest. "I have something to do here, Will. You know I can't force you to go away, but I won't let you do anything for me. Do you understand?"

"Mathew had no conditions."

"The hell with Mathew! I am not my brother, Will." He stopped, swallowed. "This is the third time you've been to this place, old man. When are you going to learn?"

Dix stared, then slowly pushed a grin into his wrinkles. "I can only learn what I've been taught, Orion."

The sigh was resigned acceptance without melodramatic bitterness. That, too, would be a waste of strength.

"Orion," the girl said impatiently, "what are we waiting for?"

"All right, Will," he said, "I will teach you something." Then he pointed at the android's pack. "I don't suppose you have any food in there."

Dix smiled.

Parric turned away before he smiled back. If nothing else, he thought, the old man will keep the girl happy.

The Walkway had apparently come to a gradual sloping end before the panics that had fired portions of the city and emptied it; now, however, that which had extended into the plain had collapsed and he faced the shattered opening, waiting for Courtney to tell him the way.

There were massive alloy pillars of a simple circular design that supported the first aboveground level, and above that similar legs which in turn held up the topmost road. These two had been the movers, if his tapes had been correct, while the bottom remained immobile for those who wished to walk to the shops in their districts or didn't care for the feeling of flying with their feet on the ground. At regular intervals were gently rising ramps, and Courtney took them to the first they could ascend; Parric, however, insisted they continue all the way up—the level above the middle was too much a roof and he demanded a look at the sky. She protested and appealed to a mute Dix, but they climbed, and Parric stood at the beginning, looking just east or northward, along the road to the Hive.

"I've read," he said in the chilled shadows of the buildings around them, "that this one was the fastest so you could get to your job or whatever the quickest."

"But why so fast?" she said.

He laughed and shrugged. "Look for a ghost to ask. I don't know."

"Will," she said, "was this the way you came?"

Parric spun on her. "How'd you know that?"

"You talk in your sleep, remember?"

"Was," Dix said. "Maybe. I don't remember."

Liar, Parric thought; you never forgot a thing in your life.

What he saw, then, was an unswerving stretch of what had once been black, was now a pale mottled grey under the half century of dust that filtered down through the jaws left in the curved glass canopy. They were standing on a concrete platform he assumed had been a waiting station where people marked time until a break in the flow permitted them descent onto the moving highway—and he noted along the left side a pair of narrower belts, starters so pedestrians wouldn't be toppled when they shifted to the main concourse.

There seemed to be a constant light wind he thought should have kept the dust clear, but it only eddied and gathered and spread weakly at their feet. Here and there were rocks apparently thrown from the windows high above them, and pieces of shattered furniture, piles of clothing whose origins his stomach refused to examine.

"It's worse on the bottom," she said when she saw what his glances were avoiding. "Sometimes it's hard to find food. The rats—Baron's rats—they don't know how to use the things the city has. Sometimes they don't want to leave because they're afraid. So . . ." and she gestured to the walls where panels between thin metal studs had been knocked out.

Parric moved to one such hole and looked down—it was still dark below, and probably never in more than twilight when the lamps weren't on. The space between Walkway and buildings was just wide enough.

"Why not you?" he asked, turning back and following her and Dix as they lowered themselves to the road.

"I don't know. I was too frightened, I guess." She hugged herself and stood close to him. "If they hadn't

148

chased me so hard, I might have. Or, if I'd stopped to think. I don't know. I just didn't.''

''Good,'' Dix said, but when she turned to him he said nothing more.

Despite the passage of time, most of the road was in fair condition. Another monument to foresight, Parric thought: build things that last forever even if we're not around to use them.

They were able to move swiftly, the solid feeling beneath them a decided advantage when they considered the pitfalls of the mountain trails. The sun posted rapidly, and the sky jammed between the towering roofs was a sharp blue and biting to the eyes raised frequently to it.

''Why are you looking up so much?'' Courtney said after he'd stumbled several times.

His grin was sheepish. ''I have to keep reminding myself it's still there.''

Occasionally, they were forced to detour to the gloom of the second level when the disarray of the flight was too high or too imaginatively gruesome for them to penetrate. And from time to time they discovered section belts still in operation, an endless rolling like a river with no place to go. At first Parric was suspicious, then little more than cautious; it would seem, he decided, that there were too few left to turn everything off, and what had been moving continued to do so until either its machinery wore out, broke down or, as Courtney reminded him, was sabotaged by those who didn't know what they were destroying. So it was, and he was thankful for the moments of automated respite he'd already been given—this, at least, no wooded forest had been able to provide.

Twilight lay in the artificial valley while the sky held its color. Parric was glad that Dix was with them; the old man kept the girl company, telling her of the way things had been from his birth in an experimental Town to his escape with Parric's grandfather. He offered nothing of the deaths he had witnessed, and Parric was grateful she had sense enough not to ask. Not yet. Not while they passed the tombs of a population. And in a manner too odd for him to untangle, he felt somewhat cheated that he had no stirrings, no desire to step off the road and explore the past. The past he had seen and was seeing was sufficiently dead to sate his curiosity, sufficiently withered to keep him from straying.

Yet he couldn't resist gawking, couldn't fend off long moments that stretched into hours of trying to reconstruct silently what had once been where he now was. The masses of people using the Walkways to travel, to visit, to attend to daily survival. The number was inconceivable; the most he had seen together at any one time was at the wedding of a Central leader much loved and honored. That a hundred, a thousand, perhaps a million times that number could be jammed into this space defeated him, and at the same time made him wonder what the Central's ContiGov remains would do with the 'plex if they could get their hands on it.

Burn it, he thought, like everything else.

They spent the night beneath one of the platforms. Courtney slept immediately. Parric sat facing the direction they'd left, half hoping to see nothing more than the black night tunnel, half hoping Wister would come cockstrutting along, right into the blades of the daggers he'd forged. It was possible, however, that the old man would be gone for some time; for all his hatred of Parric and what he stood for, Wister might have trouble getting his people to enter the city. If his teachings were any good at all, he might even have to come in alone.

Parric grinned and leaned back against a post. If that were the case, he just might start believing in a kind of divine justice. He snapped a finger against a boot, then grabbed at it, shoved a hand down alongside his leg, yanked it out—empty. The dagger was gone, and he groaned at the memory of it falling into the trench where he'd thrown it in anger that morning. He slapped his knee in disgust at his stupidity, froze when he felt the touch of metal across the back of his hand.

"You tried to stab a wall with it," Dix said. "You might need it."

Parric fumbled it back into its sheath. "Will," he said, "why did you go with Mathew?" It wasn't what he wanted to ask, but the night would permit no other question.

"Had to. He's the only one besides your grandfather who liked my singing."

"That's no answer, Will."

"Needed me, too. We got to that village, I had to show the people I wasn't a monster. They sure were surprised."

The quiet laughter made Parric smile.

"Did you help him, Will?"

The silence was a shrug.

"Now it's my turn, right?"

"Depends. Maybe. Depends."

"On what, old man? What are you going to do if you have to carry another Parric back to Central? No! Don't answer that, Will. I didn't meant it."

"You did," the voice said. "And it's fair. But I can't tell you, Orion. No matter what you think, your grandfather didn't make me a god."

He puzzled at that until he fell asleep, awoke feeling oddly bewildered and, as they rode at a pace slightly faster than he could trot, suddenly worried. Luck was a product of mind over mind, and this sudden easy trip toward the end of the journey made him uneasy. He kept looking to Courtney, but her expression gave him no clues she was thinking the same. If anything, he thought, she was becoming more and more somber, no longer pointing to the rainbows of the walls, the diamond glitters that stung them

151

from piles of glass. When Dix tried to continue a story begun the day before, she snapped at him, and Parric decided to leave her alone.

The speed of the road was uneven—creating its own wind, or child-crawl slow.

A sudden echoing shriek and it stopped. Courtney lost her balance and fell heavily to her hands and knees. Parric rode the slight bucking and glared dead ahead. A brief thought that this would result in a delay for Wister didn't cheer him.

"I'm hungry," she said without getting up.

Dix moved away to watch the road.

Parric dropped his pack into his hands and dug out half of what was left of the 'stiks. Dividing them equally, he tossed her share at her feet, then squatted and nibbled, trying to convince his stomach that there would be a day when it would really be filled and not given a simulation.

"Well," he said finally "it looks like we walk again."

She said nothing.

"When?" he said. "I keep looking up ahead there for some kind of a sign, a turn, but I can't tell. When, Courtney?"

"Tomorrow," she said when his stare forced her to answer. "Midday, maybe, if we're not stopped."

His laugh was more a bark. "Stopped by what?"

She rolled to sit and drew her knees to her chest. Dust had lightened her black shift, settled in damp streaks over her face—and she was as he'd first seen her: unattractive, harsh, bitterness corrosive beneath her flesh.

"Come on, girl, stopped by what?"

Suddenly, Dix shouted a warning.

An explosion. A crack, like wood against wood, and a shattering of glass over their heads. Dix was on them, shoving the girl aside, away from the cutting fall, while Parric turned on his heels with the pack between his feet and one dagger in his hand. Turning, and all the walls in all their colors and blindness turned with him, mocking with their impenetrability. He looked back along the Walkway, and there was a slight haze as the wind lifted the dust and spilled it in slowgrey falls through the gaps in the glass wall, over the worn lips of the platforms. He looked up, and there were great patches of clouds that scuttled over the roofs and tipped them, made them drop in hulking slow motion. He looked ahead, and there was the dust; and Willard, nodding to say he'd been through this before—and Courtney, cowering on the sidebelts, her arms trembling, her lips quivering, and a clear line of spittle dropped from the corner of her mouth.

Damning his forgetfulness, he crawled over to her, prodding when she wouldn't respond, searching for a wound, a cut, but there was none. He held her, still turning his head, then looking down at his blade, a useless gleaming fashion of metal slicing through the air.

He dropped it into its sheath, patted the boot and sat.

"Stopped by that, right?"

"Baron," she stammered. "His men. Come to find us."

"Will?" he said without looking around.

"Sooner now, but the same," the old man said.

He waited, silent, before standing and stretching. No more explosions. Only the wind, and the citysounds of the dead.

"Yes," he said quietly. Dix moved to squat in front of him, nodding. "Wister," Parric said, and punched himself on the thigh. "He did it before, Will, and he's done it again."

"Done what?" Courtney said. "He's days behind you said."

"Days behind, an hour behind, it makes no difference. He's called Baron and warned him we were coming. Li'e
153

he called Baron and warned him Dorin and Will were coming. Gave him the time to set up the ambush. To kill him. Like he wants to kill us."

Courtney snared his waist and pulled him back down, away from the old man who had raised one hand. She pressed her head against his chest and tried to hook his eyes with her own. "He will, Orion, he'll do it. He knows this place, and he knows where we're trying to go. He won't let us get there. We . . . could go back. Or get off the 'way and stay in one of the buildings. People lived there, you know. There must be some places we could stay."

He took her hands and engulfed them, forced them to her stomach and held them. "You told me he didn't like coming across this river you mentioned."

"He doesn't, he doesn't!"

"Then whatever that was, was only a warning. Unless Wister had time to tell him the whole story—which I doubt—he must think we're Outfolk and would be afraid of anything alive in here. He won't try to kill us, girl, until it's too late."

When he could see she was struggling to believe him, he repeated himself and released her hands, slowly. And slowly they separated, rose, pulled at her lower lip, her chin, settled. She sighed, and they gripped each other's shoulders and rose to their feet. Walked, swiftly, the android trailing like an aged shadow.

Twice more before nightfall they were sniped at, but they didn't stop, suppressing outward show of cringing at the falling glass, the puffs of raised dust where the glittering shards landed. A tacit pact of watchfulness kept her eyes ahead, seeking out the weakened sections of Walkway where great strips of belting had been torn up, damaged by fire, buckled under pressure of the seasons. The rubble increased. Boxes, cylinders, chairs, several tables; clothing that disintegrated at a touch, makeshift clubs, a ContiGard helmet alone and dully red. Glimpses in the wake of a rising wind of nightwhite sticks, globes, ladders of ribs. The obstacles were greatest at the Sectors' intersection avenues, indicating the press of the fleeing, and the failure and the futility. She guided him past it all with one hand wiping nervously at her mouth.

Dix moved up to the midpoint, an inconsequential position that Parric knew was an underscoring of the android's nebulous ranking in the trio. He was still vulnerable to flashes of rage at the old man's appearance, and still confused because he still didn't know what to do about it, if in fact anything should be done.

He kept himself last, looking up and behind. Watching the cityplex collapse, drop away from them and fade into cairns. Dorin had been here, and Parric spent vain minutes hunting for footprints, a half-eaten 'stik, any sign at all that his father had passed. Once, he thought to call out to Will, changed his mind in case the android could help him. And after the last sniper warning, he had to caution himself against the delusion he was invulnerable; he had spotted nothing at all, and reminded himself it was the grace of his enemy that kept him living. Grace. He grew cold. What control he had fashioned of the man called Parric was slipping from his grasp. He'd been reduced to a target to be toyed with, poked at, set to scurrying from side to side like a fish in a netted trap. There was nothing he could do to alter it, nothing he could shout, no curse he could conjure to drive off the invisible demons who were chipping at his soul. And then . . . he was a child being stalked by his elders around the houses at night, afraid that each turn at a corner would bring a shadow leaping in front of him, screaming and loosening his bowels in fear.

Clouds settled a shifting lid over the city, and he eased Courtney's shivering by digging out his cloak, folding it in half and pressing it over her shoulders. She protested, but he told her to keep her silence; he would make himself warm when the proper time came.

They walked until darkness became dangerous. At the next platform they rested, ate the last of the food, drank the last of the water. The pack had shrunk, collapsing in upon itself, and Parric hefted it and wondered what had happened to all the weeks he'd been gone. To here, he thought, coming to here, in this place, at this time. It was a letdown, and he was annoyed; he'd expected, rather, a surging of energy and the reemergence of high purpose with which he'd set out. He wanted to locate a pinnacle, ascend it and preach to the world of its evils and what they had done to his family.

A question nagged him as he stared at Will's back: which family?

Night was absolute. Stars were hidden by thunderheads racing in from the unseen sea. A keening slipped in through the breaks in the Walkway dome, and he made himself nervous by imagining footsteps, breathing, whispered conversations just beyond the reach of his hearing. He was tempted to take out the torch he'd confiscated from the Hunter but he was prey enough and didn't need to daub himself with a mark at which Baron's men could aim.

He was alone.

Dorin was gone. His grandfather and his histories were gone. Judith his mother was irretrievably vanished from the fold of his arms. And Mathew and Chamra and Willard . . .

Willard.

Bearer of the Parric dead. A failed guardian watching a family stumble into its grave. That Mathew still lived had to be chance; but Parric would not allow his life to be governed by such chances.

"Will," he said, and heard the scraping as the android moved toward him. He wanted a light so he could see the old man's eyes. "Will, I want you to go ahead. Now. You don't need the sleep. You don't need . . . just go ahead and . . . and look for traps, ambushes, Will, and things

156

like that.'' His voice became harsh, sand over glass. "Look for them, Will, and wait for us if there's nothing. Just . . . don't cross that bridge. Don't.''

There was no response but the rustling of clothes, the softly fading footfalls that refused to echo beneath the Walkway dome. A moment's deep breath was caught in the act of summoning him back, and he cursed himself for something his anger called weakness.

He was alone.

His left hand reached out. It rested on Courtney's shoulder and instantly she was beside him, her arm about his waist, her cheek to his bicep. He took the cloak and flapped it full open, wrapped it tentlike until only their faces were exposed to the air.

"Why did you do that?'' she said.

"What?''

"Send Will away. You know, I thought that his not being . . . well, not being . . .''

"Human,'' he said. "It's not a curse.''

"I didn't mean it to be, Orion! It's just that he seems so real, and he does want to help you and you're going to need it, you know. Why did you send him—''

"Courtney, drop it, please. If I knew all the answers, I'd be a god, for Plague's damned creation. I just don't want him around for a while, okay? He confuses me, if you must know. You do too, for that matter.''

Keening.

"If you want,'' she said, "you can have me. I don't think I'd mind.''

"I don't think I could,'' he said, and felt her nodding. He was grateful. An odd woman this, who had been taken and abused and booted into mud. But she kept coming back (like Will/shut up), remolding, redefining, and though he thought he knew her more inside than out, he knew too she was a stranger who had latched onto his shadow in hopes that some of the blood he was planning to spill would fall her way. Cleansing. Something. He wasn't sure what.

"How will you do it tomorrow?" she said when the wind died sufficiently for her to be heard.

"I haven't thought of it," he said honestly. "It depends on how it will be."

"If not Will, are you going to let me help?"

"Haven't you done enough already? You've brought me here, away from Redlin; you're going to bring me into the Hive and show me Baron. What more can you do, girl?"

She giggled, smothered it with her hands. "Let me have one of the knives."

"Bloodthirsty!" he said in mock surprise. "I thought you were only a tame little guide who liked to wait on people, give them baths when they're unconscious, things like that. You'd be very popular back in old Central, you know. A thing like that could catch on quickly."

She shoved at him but didn't break the cloak's protection. "You do your own catching."

"Now who's playing at words?"

"You're making fun of me."

He wished he could see if she was joking, decided to keep silent. It would be a poor time now to make a mistake.

The wind. A flat drumming as rain fell into the city, through the broken canopy and into the dust, onto the open graves they'd passed and avoided. It fell against the platform, and he felt as though they were in a small hut. He leaned back against the wall, stretched out his legs and was closing his eyes to the hypnotic storm when he heard a break in its rhythm. Courtney had stiffened. He cupped a hand to his ear and tried to siphon recognition through the rain, made out the skittering slide of a piece of city debris.

158

His first thought—Dix—was discarded without debate. The noise began to his right, passed carefully in front and paused some distance away to the left. They were tired of playing, he decided, and were looking for the easiest way to kill—the kill under cover where the bodies wouldn't be seen in rain and darkness. Muffling his own movements, he slipped the torch from his waistband and handed it to Courtney. Her fingers wouldn't grasp it and he shoved it roughly against her until she had it. Then he dropped the cloak from their arms and guided her in a sweeping motion, stopping only when she nodded and made the motion on her own. He waited until a distant thunderclap had multiplied its grumbling, then crawled to the edge of the platform. The sounds beneath the storm had ceased, but he was sure there was more than one stalking betrayal. He dropped a hand to his feet and carefully brushed it through the dust until he had uncovered what might have been a small stone. He picked it up, threw it, then darted back and jabbed at her. His head was down when the torch burst on, and he had to force himself to raise it slowly so as not to be blinded. Somehow she had managed to widen the beam, but in its first pass in a broad arc in front of them he saw nothing but the irregular falls of rain and the puddles that shot back the light. She moved swiftly, however, and at the left of the second pass he saw three shapes darting away, not bothering to hide, running only. They were just at the fringe of the pinning white. Wraiths in tatters. Hunched in expectance of a rearward attack.

"Turn it off," he said, his voice underlining the weariness of the game; and when the darkness returned, he slumped beside her and rubbed at his knees.

"Did they know we were here?" She wasn't afraid.

"Probably. Maybe not exactly, but they must have known we were somewhere around."

"Then why didn't they kill us, Orion? It doesn't make

sense. If they knew, then they had a chance and all they did was sneak around like rats trying to get into the Hive for food.''

"I'll tell you," he said. "They think we've been warned and are probably trying to decide if we should keep going or not. I think they decided to gamble on exposing themselves, deliberately making enough noise to be heard over the storm.''

"They wanted to scare us?" she said incredulously.

"Why not?"

"But if their guns didn't scare us, why should this?"

"Why should anything? How should I know, girl? I'm just guessing, and all I know is, they could have taken those guns of theirs and gotten you when the light was on. But they didn't. All they did was run.''

"Maybe they're trying to get us to follow them. Surprise us or something.''

"No," he said, "and don't ask why. I have a feeling we scared them as much as they . . . disturbed us.''

"You were scared," she accused, her delight in his failing too intense to be hidden.

He laughed and jabbed at her ribs. "A little nervous, okay?''

"They'll be even more scared when they meet Will out there. They thought there were three of us here, remember?" She grabbed his hand, massaged the back. "Will he kill them, Orion?''

Parric stared into the darkness. "No," he said. "No. It may not have sounded like it, girl, but that old man and me have an understanding. He won't kill them.''

She stopped the rubbing, pulled the hand to her lap. "You don't like him here, do you?''

He didn't answer.

"Well, I do. I think he's nice. He talks as much as I do.''

"He never used to.''

160

She laughed. "With you for company, who would want to?"

He yanked back his hand, she snatched for it, trapped it and held it to her cheek. "They know we're not scared of them now, don't they, Orion?"

"They know it, girl," he said. "And they know I'll keep coming."

X

PHILAYORK! Consider the very name itself as your gourmand diction passes it round your urban palate. It is an evocation of heartbeats without number, all linked to the pulse of throbbing humanity. It is a celebration, moreover, of the great glass-skinned Walkways that join the sparkling Sectors and dance to the tune of twenty-four-hour laughter and tears, birth and death. The vaulted exaulted Hives of Commerce dispensing the workers to the great and storied Unities of the Globe: Eurecom, Panasia, Nordsland—even to the Exotic underside Confederation of Ausland.

PHILAYORK!

Disdainfully dwarfing the eternal waves of the magnificent sea. Powerful. Dynamic. The very spine of our ContiGov's posture in the sprawling Universe.

Our City—Your City—The ONLY City worth—

"Universe?" Parric stared closer at the tattered promolet to be sure his eyes weren't simply juggling the words to suit his mood. But *Universe* is what it said, and he crumpled the plaspulp propaganda into a ball and tossed it aside without looking to see where it had landed. Courtney had discovered it jammed into a recess formed by a battered portion of the road, had asked him shyly if he would read it to her. It was the first time he had known she hadn't the skill herself, and he was amazed that she had been able to survive this long without it—until he remembered that she had little if any need at all to piece out the songs of man's consummate vanity. So he had read it, and she had listened, her face creased in a frown, then softened into disinterest. He finished it only for his own amusement.

"Is that what they used to think about the city?" she said.

"Some did, I suppose," he answered. "And some didn't." He glanced around at the quiet destruction and shrugged. "Obviously, not enough did, right?"

She didn't reply, only grabbed the ends of his cloak and pulled them tightly across her chest. It was chilly despite the return of blue sky, and the wind continued to dart at them from the Walkway breaks. They'd been traveling since dawn at an erratic pace that had them running one moment, and dawdling the next. Parric couldn't make up his mind how fast to bring the end to him; the anticipation had become a dry taste in his mouth, a goad at the base of his spine—and he grinned often at nothing but the feeling.

Yet that same anticipation tethered his stride. It was not a prolongation to add a sweetness to the culmination, but rather an unpleasant hesitation in a renewed doubt that what he had to do, had to be done. And it was wrong to feel that way; he had been too close to his own demise too often for doubts to gain hold now. There were no doubts, he told himself. There were none at all, and he was a fool for risking his concentration on trivial mental obstacles.

There had been no further incidents from Baron's men, no other attempts to frighten them off, no direct attacks to injure or kill them. The Walkway directly ahead was deserted, and unnaturally clean; swept by hand, he thought, to give a clear view to anyone waiting, and watching, and aiming their weapons. He knew that the tension of suspense had been created only in his mind, knew it, and let it boil acid in his stomach. And he paused often, once stopping to rub at his abdomen in hopes the

163

burning would fade and be replaced by the rocksteady nerves he'd thought he had trained himself to have. All those days in the pits learning about combat self-defense, all the nights in his rooms slashing at his wall shadows— reflex had been what he was seeking, a Rogue-like mind-lessness that would keep him alive until his blades became bloody.

And in part, upon reflection, it had all worked. In part, however, because he hadn't counted on the seedling doubts, or the quiet moments afterward when he tried and failed to bury the bodies he had caused to exist.

The loose sleeves of his shirt flapped against his ribs like banners black and stiff. His eyes squinted to fight the wind, and his hair was pushed back from his forehead, pulling at the roots. Courtney had tucked her face close to her chest, but he refused to look away. He'd rather the tears be swept from his cheeks than miss a single moment of what was his due.

And ahead: a brilliant explosion of steadily glaring light, erasing the buildings as they marched dead and empty into it. The Walkway faded, the sky dipped. It was like an open furnace of white, and he would not ask the girl to explain its source.

Noon, and they stopped. Courtney couldn't keep herself still; she shifted her weight from one foot to the other, standing slightly behind and to Parric's right, wanting the constant wind blocked and not wanting to miss a word, an expression, a single blink of his eye. He knew this, but would not look down to her. Instead, he dropped the pack at her feet and walked forward. Slowly. His arms lifted away from his waist, his fingers and palms open to the air. Testing. Searching.

The bridge.

A blackened tongue carrying carnage into the mouth of the city. No cleansing here. Slats, sacks, bits of cloth, shards of leather. Pressed against the thick tubular railings

164

untouched by rust. Echoes of screams. No memories of laughter. Most of the glass had been broken, and what was left of the canopy were the spidered frames that webbed black against the sky.

He walked to one side and looked down, crossed and looked over the opposite side. To the river. Sparkling, rushing, like a white comet's tail. He picked up a section of broken piping and tossed it over, watched its spiral, lost its splash in the glare of the water. It was a long time in falling.

He walked slowly back to the center of the road and lifted a hand to shade his eyes. From the windows: rectangles, squares, massive great circles catching the image of the sun a millionfold and shooting it back like the dizzying lights of a gigantic computer. There were no clouds to dim them, and he was forced to turn away, then back again to dare that his eyes be blinded. Scanning to rooftops that were peaked, domed, leveled as though thick fingers had been sliced off at the joint. Tinted, bleached, the backdrop of dreams he knew he never could have had from the pictures he'd seen.

A footstep, and he didn't turn.

"It was here," he said quietly to the girl at his side. "I know it was, but I can't see any of the bodies."

She released the cloak to become wings behind her back. "I remember a couple of times people would come," she said, "and he would meet them here. He didn't want them in the Hive. He said they would contaminate us if we let them in. There were fights. Every time, he would win, and then he would have the dead thrown into the river. He didn't want his enemies sneaking up on him, pretending they'd been killed."

He nodded, accepting without sentiment the fact that he would have no relics to return to the families in Town Central. Nothing would be left—no weapons, no clothing, and the rain would have long ago washed the road clean of their blood. He walked halfway across the link to the Hive and once again stared down at the river. Courtney remained on the road proper, her pack still hugged tightly to her chest. And when he turned back to her, he saw the look: a child wanting and not daring to run from its parent. He stretched out a hand and, when she balked, shook it until she approached him and dropped the pack at his feet. He knelt and ripped it open, tossing aside the last of the provisions. Then he pulled out a small bundle, and the handgun.

The wind caught at the packshell, lifted it, scaled it, and Parric didn't turn to watch it drift over the railing to the chasm.

He stood, took the weapon and handed it to her, closed her fingers around it gently when she shook her head.

"You'll need it," she protested. "I don't know how to use it."

"Don't worry, I'll show you." He became stern. "You've been waiting for this, haven't you? You've wanted this, isn't that right? Well, don't you think it's about time you joined me?"

A band of brown leather halved the bundle. He took out a dagger and sliced it through, tossing it aside and ignoring its flutter scurrying after the packshell. Then he grabbed the cloth and held it up for the wind to unfurl. It was of a green that only mountains can mix when the moon is high; a cloak too short that hung just above his knees. Carefully, he shook it to banish its folds, then placed it around his shoulders and fastened it at his neck with a silver-and-red clasp.

"Is it some kind of ceremony you do, back at that Central place?" Courtney said, reaching out to touch the soft material.

"It was Dorin's," he said simply. "They were going to bury him in it."

He grinned, closed it around him, let the wind take it

open again, and his daggers were in his hands. "It also has a few places here and there where things can be put." He laughed as she stared, trying to see how he replaced the blades. He repeated the move, and sobered. "You see, this cloak, girl, could have saved his life. But he was ambushed here and never got to use it. But you and I know that Wister has already let this Baron in on our trip. We won't be ambushed."

"Maybe he's catching up," she said nervously.

"Oh, he's doing that, all right. He'd be a total idiot if he didn't. The question is: how badly does he want us dead? Bad enough to let this other little duke do it for him? Or so bad that we're only targets for some sort of holding action until he can finish the job himself."

"That one," she said when he stopped. "We've made him too mad now. Before, it was all right if Shem or Lynna did it. But he won't want anyone else to do it now. I know him. That's the way it will be."

"In that case," he said, "why don't we get moving? The view is nice, but . . ." and he gestured for her to lead the way. She hesitated, then lifted her chin and began picking her way through the piles of debris blatantly purposeful in their arrangements against shifting by the weather. At her insistence he'd taken back the handgun and, although he knew it was nearly drained of its charge, held it at the ready. The bridge was a perfect place for a small band to hide—secreted amid all the reminders of something not to be remembered; no one just looking would anticipate an attack from piles of the dead.

Slowly, cautiously, freezing at every sudden movement, waiting until their breathing returned to normal before continuing. Parric cursed the wind for concealing any footsteps or blunders he might have been able to hear, but knew it worked the same in his favor and tried to hold that thought whenever he felt his hands growing slick with perspiration, or his back protesting the unnatural crouch he'd twisted it into; one step at a time, he cautioned himself, so you don't fall flat on your face.

A shadow at the bridge's end. A sweep of his arm pushed the girl to the safety of an upturned carton. It was Dix, and he thought the old man was preparing to stop him from entering the Hive. There was a moment's brief shame that he'd not thought of the android since the night he'd sent him away, shame that increased and vanished as he glanced over his shoulder at the expanse just passed. The rubble. The ghosts of the ambush, the spectres of the dead. Willard had not died here and so he had not stayed, leaving the bridge for Parric to see, to feel. The cloak flared up and slapped against his face; he pushed it away, the cloth smooth and cool against his sliding palm. His fingers reached up to grasp the silvered clasp, and were stayed when the girl grabbed his wrist and pulled him forward until the bridge had ended.

Dix closed a hand on his arm and turned him around. He pointed—there, and there, and there again—without speaking. From the tightly closed lips came a faint humming, a noteless melody that Parric recalled from the burial of his father.

"You do feel, don't you?" he said.

"As I can, Orion. As I can."

"I told you," Courtney said, stepping between them. "He's real."

Indeed, Parric thought, and I should be damned for thinking otherwise.

He grinned. The old man shrugged, reached out and made a meaningless adjustment to the folds of the cloak.

"Mathew . . ." he began.

"Forget him," Parric said without rancor. "You're with me now. It's still not all right."

At the bridge's end, the Walkway changed: it dipped slightly, narrowing the distance between levels, trimming several meters from its width. Intersections were closer, and there were more intermediary exits leading steeply down to the stationary street at ground level. And unlike the deliberate blindness of Sectors just passed, there were windows that tossed his ghost from pane to pane and prevented him from seeing inside. The rubble, too, was less evident as though the businessmen and government drones in the Hive had less to take with them, or had taken it all with them before the rest of the population had caught the panic. Privileges of the mighty, he thought—and disliked himself for hoping for a third alternative, that the Hive had been the first stricken so that flight was impossible because the dead couldn't run.

At each station exit were pairs of comunit hoods, but when he headed for one not wrenched from its foundation, Courtney stopped him.

"Some of them still work," she warned, "and Baron keeps a team checking. Try it now and you'll give us away."

"They probably know already," he reminded her, "but okay."

Less than a kilometer from the bridge's end she took them to the bottom level. He wanted to question, but he was in her territory now and didn't have much room for strong argument.

The street, despite the afternoon hour, was already in dusty twilight. The transystem's massive pillars were grey and functional, lacking any attempts to disguise or beautify their presence. Globes fastened to the underside of the middle Walk had been shattered, as were the curve-necked lamps jutting from the buildings over each doorway—and there were dozens, no two alike although all were outlined in the same burnished alloy that had not lost its mirror gleam. It wasn't difficult for him to imagine the resulting indirect illumination when the lights had been working; a constant carnival, he thought, and the immediate danger of his position faded somewhat as he poked into shops, offices, rooms whose functions he was unable to determine. There was little left in any of them, looting and fire apparently completing the evacuation.

"Did you ever come down here?" he asked as they stared through one jagged plate window.

"Sometimes," she said. "Once or twice, I found some clothes that hadn't been taken. Mostly, though, there wasn't anything, and most of the dials and things I don't know how to work. What was gone before I came was left up there," and she pointed to the Walkway.

He groped for a remark to lighten her mood, glanced at Dix who shook his head. Her nervousness was finally cracking her control and he was angry that she doubted his ability to protect her; but he checked himself with a reminder that she'd been marked for execution once before in this place, and now she was again, only because she was with him. He took her hand and led her to the center of the darkening street, away from the shops, the offices, the humps of rotted clothing that marked the fall of those who hadn't been successful learning how to forage in a largely mechanical forest.

Another kilometer, and he felt her sag against him, fighting the weakness and unable to contain it. Food, he thought, and turned his attention back to the doorways, hoping they might locate themselves a miracle in the form of a restaurant whose supplies hadn't been ravaged.

Her hand tightened.

"Do you want to rest a minute?"

She shook her head and pulled him to a halt. "I don't like it down here," she said, "but I still think I saw something up there."

At the same moment, Dix bent over and picked up a stone, walked back to make a show of its size.

"Men," he said, and Parric nodded, moving the two of them as casually as he could to the nearest pillar and walked behind it. As he did, there was a crack and a whine as a cloud of stone chips exploded off the nearest wall. He ducked involuntarily, yanking the girl to him while Dix shucked his useless pack.

"What's up?" Parric asked.

"Men. They can't hurt me, if I'm lucky," and Dix patted his hips.

"You can't. They think you're human, old man. You'll be dead for sure if they find out otherwise."

A second shot was no nearer, nor was a third, and Parric relaxed and straightened. Projectiles, he thought, and was thankful that Baron's men, unlike Wister's, hadn't gotten hold of the military laser. Somehow he imagined this would work to his advantage, but when a fourth shot kicked up dust and rubble less than a meter from his foot, he was unable to think of what that might be.

"How many, Will?"

"Couldn't see all that clear. No more than two, I think."

"All right," he said, and settled the handgun over his fist. He bent and chanced a look down the tunnel-like street, seeing nothing but perspective close the Walkway shut at the near horizon. Dark shapes hulked in piles. The trail of the dying wind marked in dust.

He slid his right palm over the sensorload on the gun's triangle and shook his head. His daggers and Will's strength would be more useful now, more effective; he estimated a less than ten-second bolt, or two at four if his targets were spread and running. After that, the laser would be just as much a remnant as the city he was in.

"The intersection," Courtney whispered suddenly into his ear.

Two men, small and husky, darted across the street and hid themselves behind a ramp before he could fire. They were angling, keeping to the shadows, using the shop doors for cover as they sought the range of their weapons.

One hundred meters, and one of them fired, though the shot fell short and far to their left. Parric raised the laser, aimed over the notched sights and waited until they attempted another break. But when he felt the warming pulse in his hand and saw the light trail of smoke where his shot had scorched one of the distant pillars, he dropped the gun and stood. Stepped into the road. Ignored Courtney's shrill cry of alarm.

With Wister the advantage of Dorin's techprim whirl was somehow different, and the use of the laser acceptable and proper. Now, however, he felt oddly in the wrong. There was something about the way the men ran, a limping gait that bespoke bravado in the cloud of dying . . . it was stupid, decidedly unnatural, but he felt without thinking that what he had set himself out to do would not be sanctioned by the advantage he had.

A shadow disturbed him, and Dix was at his side. Parric spat, wanted to shove him away before realizing Dix was exaggerating his stoop, the angle of his head—arrogance, then, and senility to breed overconfidence. He shook his head just enough for Will to see, and smiled. He had time for one question: "Was it this way with Dorin?"

Another shot spit dust a hand's breadth from his boot, and the man on the left tossed away his weapon, pulled from beneath his shirt a blade as dim as the light through which he ran. Parric watched him directly, setting himself as they slowed, apparently disconcerted. They both wore dark shirts, dark trousers too small and too old to be even marginally impressive. Their feet were booted by cloth wrappings, and several tag ends slapped at their calves. This can't be an army, Parric thought, and would have called out, wanted to call out to halt their rush, but they flung themselves wildly and he braced to be toppled, was, but more because of his surprise at their almost total lack of strength. And in falling he saw a fist connect with Willard's jaw, saw Willard sag and collapse and lie still in

172

the dust. He had no time to think but shoved one man off his chest with only a single blow of his forearm; the other kicked at Will's side and threw himself at Parric's feet, clinging until Parric sat up, twisted and kicked him aside. They returned, arms already punching the air as though momentum alone would penetrate his defenses and bring him down again. The bladed one feinted, charged, and Parric snared his wrist easily, lifted and threw him over his shoulder. A shout cut off by a pain-filled moan, and the second man dove for Parric's knees, knocking him backward while Parric punched at the top of his head. A freeze, and he felt as if he was wrestling with the youngsters back in Central, with no harm meant and little harm done. But the weakened man was trying to climb his legs like a ladder, one clawed set of fingers grasping for his throat. Parric fell onto his back, raised his knees and awkwardly dumped him past his head. He turned on his knees, crawled and sat on the man's chest.

"All right, you Winded damn fool," he said, more impatient than angry.

The man spat and Parric slapped him, meeting bone instead of flesh. Saw the emaciation and fatigue and years of hiding turn the face to an animated shroud. The eyes were fear-wide, darting from side to side while Parric held the hands pinned beside the head, bending away from the legs that tried to kick feebly.

"Will you stop it, you Plagued idiot!" he said sharply.

The man did, abruptly, and after a moment's staring, Parric stood, backing away with hands on hips. The first man was lying in a crumpled mass of rags at the base of a pillar, his back oddly humped for the position he was in. Courtney was kneeling beside him. She slipped a hand under his chest, drew it back quickly and held up a blood-stained palm.

"Your friend is dead," Parric said to the man still puffing, still lying on his back. "Why don't you and I take a few deep breaths and calm down some. Then maybe we can talk a little.''

"I'll kill you.'' It was an old man's voice trying not to cry.

"No, I'm sorry, but you won't.''

Suddenly the man rolled away and came up with a jagged knife of splintered glass. Parric shook his head, held out his palms to ward off the idea. But the man came at him, stumbling, and Parric sidestepped easily, pushing and toppling him onto his back again. He rose, wiped the back of a hand across his mouth and glanced at Courtney who was standing silently over Dix's still unmoving form. He threatened her, but she didn't move. He waved the glass blade at Parric, who only shook his head.

"Plague,'' the man said. "Plague.''

Parric frowned. Obviously this was intended to promote some sort of reaction, but his failure to respond only made the man more desperate.

"Plague!'' and it was a shout that fell back from the Walkway above.

"He wants you to think he's ill with the Plague,'' the girl said. "We did it all the time to the rats who came begging. It would frighten them away, sometimes.''

Parric turned to her. "Does he believe it?'' And when she screamed a warning, he held up a hand barely in time to check the man's rush. His fingers took the wrist with the glass, and his free hand stiffened, and he jammed its heel into the man's chin. The head snapped back as the feet slid out from under him, and he fell. Still. Another pile of rags.

Parric knelt and searched for a pulse beneath the grime. He lay both his hands alongside the man's head and felt the unfettered play of the spine. Then he rose, toed the shard of glass away from the body and brought his heel down on it, once, twice, a dozen times until his leg ached. He walked stiffly away, kept on moving until Dix and the girl ran up beside him; he touching his shoulder, she taking his hand.

"Is that the way you helped Dorin, old man?"

"If I am an old man, I can't be young, too. Besides, you said you wanted to do it yourself. You did. Yourself."

"Great," Parric said. "Brave, wasn't it? The mighty Orion against a pair of half-starved men."

"They would have killed you," Dix said flatly.

"I didn't have to kill them, though. I could have knocked them unconscious. Tied them up, sat on that idiot's chest until he told me what I have to know. I didn't have to kill them, Will."

"They were dying anyway," the girl said.

He stopped, shook off Will's hand and glared at her. "Is that the way you people think around here? They were dying anyway so you do it for them? What in the name of the almighty Plague goes on here?"

She watched him without flinching. "Being afraid," she said, "and believe me or not, all the men here aren't old and they're not sick." She paused and brushed a finger across her cheek. "They weren't too old to kill your Dorin."

He looked back at the two bodies, asked her to fetch the gun while he leaned against a pillar and tried to convince himself that she was right and the acid welling in his throat was a reaction only to be expected when the men he sought turned out not to be giants, but men after all.

"Something has happened," Dix said as he watched the girl running back. "They weren't like this. Not before."

Parric heard the words and saw the old man, but nothing reached him until Courtney returned and he held her until his arms stopped trembling. He kissed her forehead.

"I guess we must be close."

"We are. Two more sections and we'll be there. And there'll be others, Orion. The fighting will bring them."

She touched the clasp at his throat and he grabbed the

dirt-streaked fingers, moved them to the blond in his beard and grinned.

"For luck," he said, and when she stifled a laugh behind her free hand, and glanced over her shoulder to wink at Dix, he began to wonder just who was being revenged in all this.

Less than half an hour later Parric saw the four men, spread in an arc from shopside to shopside. They brandished metallic-looking clubs and appeared much larger than the previous two. He ordered Courtney to get behind some protection, but she refused and grabbed the handgun from him, slipping it on as deftly as if she'd been born handling it. It seemed unwieldy and comical on her small fist, but even if the remaining bolt missed, it would give the attackers pause, breaking their formation and evening the odds until he could do most of the work himself.

He smiled, and felt a surge that made him want to laugh. The old men were forgotten, only the image that they were his enemies remained as he anticipated the careful advance and moved to the opposite side of the underpass tunnel, motioning to Dix to stay with the girl. Suddenly, a shot ricochetted off the pillar some meters above his head. He spun around in time to see a fifth man dashing toward him, firing from a stiff-armed position. There was a grunt, and Dix slapped at his shoulder, dropped to the street and crawled quickly to the protection of a doorway. No smug lessons here, Parric thought as he dove straight ahead and crawled toward a low mound of debris; self-preservation only since a lucky hit could do far more than damage a synthetic arm. He waited anxiously until Will motioned that he was all right, then Courtney was beside him, her hands raised, her eyes squinting. She depressed the handgun release and there was a silence, and the man kept running, stumbling now and suddenly screaming and clawing at the side of his head. He fell heavily, and his weapon skittered from his grip. Parric moved to his knees, but the girl was ahead of him, across the open space, grabbing the gun and spinning just as another shot turned them back to the four stalking ahead.

Parric snatched at a pillar base and pulled himself around it, coming to his feet as Courtney lunged to hide behind a pillar directly opposite him. He waved, and she slid the gun across the road.

They waited.

Will was two doorways up, invisible to the attackers. Parric lifted a hand, and the android pointed to his left shoulder. A glint of metal where the shirt had been torn away. Parric closed his eyes; there was no blood, but it didn't make any difference.

And they waited.

No movement. No warnings or shouts of direction. Another shot, and close enough to give him suspicion that this man knew something of what he was doing. He scanned the gleaming shopfronts as far as he dared without risking exposure. Then he covered the ground again and grinned. He whistled once, and Courtney stared at the hand signals through the dusk, once making him laugh silently when she had to scratch her head before inspiration penetrated and she nodded eagerly. The man was on her side, and if the others held off long enough, he might be able to shorten their stay. When she whistled back, he checked his projectile weapon, allowing a moment of amazement at its apparent age; then he lifted it while she pointed, and aimed at a doorway some fifty meters from where she knelt. By checking the shopfronts, she had located a mirror movement; and when the man poked his head out, Parric fired, missing, cursing but ready when the attacker in sudden panic darted out and was cut down.

Courtney mimed applause, and Parric bowed slightly before discarding the empty, useless weapon.

It clattered, and there were echoes.

He pressed his back against the pillar, and it was cold. He stared at the rags of the man Courtney had burned. He craned, and saw Will slumped in the doorway.

Suddenly Courtney screamed, and a man raced from a doorway directly to her right, leapt and pulled her to the street. Parric, not bothering to look, darted from cover and was halfway across when a club struck him just below the knees, and his hands were out to break his fall, rolling him before he could be trapped on his back. To his knees, then, before the rest of the band was on him, and he grunted in surprise at their unexpected strength.

He caught only second-long images during the struggle that tumbled him, pummeled his thighs and cheeks, the back of his head. The faces were younger, angrier and greyly grim. He saw a fist and managed to duck away from it, a quick grin at a shout of pain when it struck the street instead of his jaw. His own fist responded blindly and one man fell off. Another, from behind, still had his arms wrapped around Parric's chest, and they rolled until they met a pillar and the grip loosened. Parric kicked out and pulled himself to his feet, pushed off when his vision cleared and smashed a boot between the legs of the man bent over the girl. There was no sound but a harsh, in-drawn breath. Courtney shoved, was on her feet, and they were running to Dix, giving him balance until he ran with them, left arm dangling, not bothering to work at confusion, running straight down the center of the street.

At a cleared access ramp, Parric veered and led them up the slope toward the second level. Courtney balked, then, and he looked up to see three men waiting, their clubs swaying at their sides.

"Down!" she shouted, and broke away from him, vaulting the low protective railing and plummeting back to the street. Parric's own hesitation and surprise allowed one of the men to toss his club, catching him a glancing blow alongside his left leg. He winced and went down on one knee, head bowed, arms hidden. When he came up again, his daggers were in his hands.

There were footsteps behind him. He spun, saw Dix using his one good arm as a ram into the stomach of a two-meter giant; the man grunted, staggered back and Dix tipped him over the railing, whirled to trip, kick and roll back down the ramp a second armed runner. A screech from below that was answered by a man's high-pitched and agonizing scream. Parric sidled to the railing and watched as Courtney held her right arm while a figure in mottled black groveled at her feet, moaning, trying to straighten his legs.

The trio at the head of the ramp began to move down, cautiously, confidently—and two more came up, hurrying, tackled Dix and the three toppled over the side. Parric lifted one leg over the railing and scythed with the daggers long enough to put pause in the attack, long enough to allow him to leap. But as he landed a club struck him full in the back and he sprawled, tumbled, came up against a shopfront with his legs out in front of him.

Courtney raced over to him, grabbed at his elbow and tried to lift him up. Nothing would respond. Not his hand, not his feet, and for a screaming moment he thought his spine might be snapped. His vision blurred and he felt one of the daggers being snatched from his hand. He heard another shout, a grunt, and the sound of a heavy body thudding against the street.

He blinked, then, and saw she had thrown the blade expertly into the neck of a weaponless man.

"Come on!" she said; and he tried, willing the numbness to vanish, pretending that the river pain that spread down toward his buttocks was only the remnant of a dream he hadn't yet shaken off. But his muscles were sluggish, his head a leaden weight atop a neck that refused to balance it. Courtney kept yanking, and the height he achieved when he finally stood was too dizzying, and he reached out for support, tripped, and slammed back against the wall.

Courtney sobbed, her frustration building to rage.

Her sobs were cut short.

Parric braced himself, then, but could not handle the three who pounced on him, dragged him down again; he could only hope they wanted him alive.

XI

So THIS IS the Praetorian, he thought sourly, the chosen protectors of a mighty minor king. They were dressed in ill-fitting assortments of tunics and blouses, and though most wore boots, they were broken and worn like Plague-diseased skin. Unshaven, uncombed, and uncaringly unwashed. The youngest was close to Parric's age, the eldest carried the unconscious Courtney over his shoulder. Dix stumbled convincingly like an old man thrashed to the edge of his grave, his arm in a makeshift sling, the shirt carefully bunched at the shoulder to keep prying eyes from learning too much—the blood, Parric thought coldly, most likely came from one of the Baron's dead. He himself was untouched and aching. They seemed not to be worried that either of the men might look for an escape, flanking them only while two silent leaders led the way from the scene of the fight. He tried to speak with them, any of them, but he was refused an answer, was not even given the satisfaction of a grunt or a nod. As if he was invisible, yet trapped within a spell of their own making.

They passed a street cleared of its rubble as far as he could see. Still another was clean, and a third was in the process. A group of people whose sex he couldn't immediately determine were slowly, weakly, sweeping everything within their reach into the dark mouths of huge drains. Only one stopped his cleaning long enough to glance up when the party passed, and when he saw what had disturbed him, he looked away again without signaling the others.

"Can I assume," Parric finally said when their footsteps in the dust made his nerves raw, "that you're taking us to Lemmy Baron?"

No one answered.

"That's all I came to see, you know. We were attacked and we had to defend ourselves."

It was a hollow lie and he knew it, and wasn't surprised when they continued to ignore him. He asked Will how he felt, and the old man smiled wryly, touched his hip casing and brushed his fingers against one cheek; once, he tried to sidle closer to the girl to see if he could bring her back to consciousness or, at the least, estimate the extent of her injuries. And it was the only time that one of them moved toward him; but he still wasn't touched, only warned with a glare that was curiously weary in its threat.

Finally, as he was ready to believe they were leaving the city entirely, they moved out from under the transystem and headed south along what must have been a primary boulevard. He resigned himself to the escort, then, and stared at the ornate designs missing from those Sectors he'd seen across the river. And this is where it was all, he thought with the false tug of nostalgia, the east coast Hive of Noram's commerce. The credivaults, the Exchanges, the dickering of computers for trade, for favors, for the price of a country. Marble twined with color-baked alloy, glass flecked with gold, plazas with dry fountains, dead trees, dead shrubs. They passed the bulbous extension of an arena whose marquee retained enough of its message to proclaim the arrival of the Panasian Team. Must have been a landmark event, Parric thought, and wondered what it was that Panasia could possibly send here that would cause such a stir; if, he added cynically, it was a stir at all and not just something to fill in the time. No Utopian euphoria here, if his grandfather was to be believed—just a bigger city with smaller people who were conditioned to their buildings and ignored the outside. Nothing spectacular, the old man had once said, just people and stone, just the way it's always been.

It was an hour before the leaders swerved into a cavern of granite and marble and great tattered banners hanging limply from a ceiling hidden in the late afternoon gloom. Along the far wall were banks of lifts and escalators, but the group avoided them, preferring instead a broad metal staircase that rose in an unhurried spiral. The man with Courtney assumed the lead position, and Parric was too busy trying not to look down to see if she'd opened her eyes, to see if Dix was holding his own. He held tightly to the bannister, his legs fighting the steps, his back patched with aches that drove final defiance back into caution. And when it was apparent they'd be climbing for a considerable distance, he stopped counting the stairs and concentrated instead on the ways he would make Baron pay for the things he had done.

Will would keep his promise; Parric would be alone.

But to do it quickly would be transparently unsatisfactory after so long a time, yet to deliberately prolong the moment of his dying would be something less than civilized, and would bring him as low as the man he sought. A chase, perhaps, or a form of hand-to-hand combat. One thing he was sure of—there would be no reprieve or a listening to mercy, nor would there be an assassination in the dark. He wanted it open. Clear. Visible. Especially to the stars blanked out by the sun. And he wanted it done before Wister arrived.

The first landing was broad, leading immediately to a wide corridor featureless and dim under lighting partially extinguished by failures in the system. What carpeting remained was worn, faded, encrusted with chunks of dirt and stale food. Gouges in the pale yellow walls marked the vandalism that had torn benches and tables from their

183

moorings; and for one short space both walls and ceiling were coated with charred shadows of some years-old fire. Behind doors of varying faded colors he could hear voices: children playing, crying, arguing with whining adults. And everywhere the stench of decayed food, excrement, urine.

He gagged and was jabbed in the back. He glared but made no move; he was staring instead at a door through which the girl was carried, Will was shoved. He balked, then, wanting more than a prisoner's entrance, but he was pushed and his hands couldn't catch him against the jamb.

The room he estimated at twenty meters square, the ceiling half as high. Sconces held flickering small bulbs, a jumble of furniture was pushed to the walls in haphazard fashion. The floor was bare, and in its center an oblong ebony table littered with plates and cups, crumbs and splinters of bone. A bald man growled an order, and for the first time, Parric noticed the people he was facing.

Mostly women and mostly half naked. Thin to the lip of starvation, hair knotted, faces lined with dirt and fear. When they saw him, when his guards stepped aside, many of them whimpered and pulled to their spindly legs what might have been children but seemed more like twisted trunks of a fire-scoured forest. Thumbs in mouths, many completely hairless, several stomachs distended grotesquely. And again the stench, but no one except himself seemed to notice.

The bald man clapped, and several ran to the table, spilling its litter onto the floor while children leapt to the crumbs and shoved them greedily into their mouths. The larger ones pushed aside the smaller, and they were all scattered when more of the women and not a few of the men waded into the scramble and cuffed them back into the crowd.

Courtney was stretched on her back, her face pale, one hand dangling over the table's edge. Parric moved to be by her side but he was stopped when a stick of a boy stood in front of him and menaced him with a jagged leg torn from a chair.

Willard was pushed up beside him. Expressionless. Rigid.

Except for an occasional whimpering, it was silent while Parric turned in a slow circle to see what he'd come to destroy. Knight, he thought, on a limping charger with rusted armor, and the dragons whose fire wouldn't scorch a leaf. He looked to Will in a silent pleading question: this couldn't be what Dorin had run into, these couldn't be the men who had caused his death, and the death of the others. There was no answer, and he decided they must be the rats the girl had warned him about, the scavengers of the city who obviously had nothing left to find.

The bald man waved, and several women hovered around the girl, hiding her from view. Then he stepped in front of the table and stared at Parric and Will. He had been heavy once, but the wattles at his neck and the sacks of limp flesh dangling from his arms made Parric turn away until the man spoke.

"You've killed a lot of us, too many men."

Parric almost choked on the arrogance. "I want to see Baron."

"We don't care for men who kill other men," the bald man said.

"Is this where I can find Lemmy Baron?"

"I remember that girl. She was supposed to die."

Parric took a step forward and felt a hand at his arm. It was too much. He reached around and pried the fingers off, bending them backward until their owner yelped and snatched the hand away. Then he looked back, saw the women and children, the scrawny old men pushing to the limits of the walls, as frightened as though he was a carrier himself. He pointed at the bald man.

"I want to see Lemmy Baron."

The bald man sputtered, wiped spittle from his chin and folded his arms over his chest. A decade ago it would have been imposing, but Parric felt only disgust and a growing disdain.

"Baron," he said. "How many times do I have to ask?"

"He's busy right now," the bald man said, some of his composure returning. "I can answer your questions, if you want. But first you must tell me who you are. Nobody comes to our . . . Baron's home without first telling us who he is. That's the way it is. You must tell me."

It was unbelievable, and Parric had to close his eyes in the hope that once reopened he would find himself back in the mountains and away from this nightmare.

"You must tell us."

But the menace was more of a plea, and Parric absently fingered the clasp of his cloak.

"If you don't tell us, we'll have to lock you away, you see. We don't like to do that, but we'll have to because you won't tell us who you are."

"How old are you?" Parric said, and there was no pleasure in the bald man's startled confusion. "I asked you how old you were. How long have you been here? Were you here three years ago?"

The bald man stepped back until his buttocks pressed against the edge of the table. He had not dropped his arms, but their attitude now was one of protection.

"You've talked to Wister, haven't you?" No answer, though it was clear enough from the stir in the room. A child began crying, stopped when a hand slapped him viciously across the mouth. Several people stared at the bald man, who nodded, and they squatted, holding the young ones between their legs and sniffling.

"You've talked to Wister, and he told you that the girl and me were to be stopped. Not killed. Just stopped.

You," and he pointed again, and the bald man flinched, "are the one he sees. You're the one he calls Yasher. Why doesn't he talk to Baron anymore? Come on, man, I've asked you enough questions for one day! Answer me. Now!"

"Who are you?" the bald man said, stubbornly frowning.

Parric lowered his head, raised it. Felt the men behind him moving away. And there was a sadness that drained his aggravation and replaced it with a vacuum. "You don't know me," he said. "My name is Parric." He paused. "Orion Parric."

Still frowning, Yasher looked to the others who refused to meet his glances, only pressed themselves tighter against the walls.

"Years ago, three, a man came with some others," Parric said, aware that he was being listened to like an elder telling a story, aware that his voice was a monotone of somber defeat. "He met with Baron and probably some of you out on the bridge, the bridge to the Hive. Only you didn't talk with him. You attacked him and his men, murdered them and threw their bodies into the river. The man and one other got away. He died before he reached home." He raised a quivering fist in accusation. "You were one of them, weren't you? You were one of the attackers on the bridge."

Standing, the bald man collapsed. His face wrinkled suddenly, as if he had been able to control the stubbled skin and had now lost the power. His mouth sucked in, his tongue flicking in the manner of one who had no teeth. The arms that hid his chest fell to his sides; his shirt was torn in several places and its seam was open to his waist. His breasts were like a woman's, his stomach a series of hair-spotted rolls.

Parric took a long step forward, and Yasher scuttled

187

around to the other side of the table, one hand still on Courtney's shoulder. The move wasn't meant to be intimidating, but Parric's harsh rasp was.

"You will tell me where Baron is, old man, and you will tell me why you killed those people."

"Tell him, Yasher," one of the women said, and she was joined by a simpering chorus which included the men who remained in pitiful guard at the door. Yasher looked betrayed, and the last of his command vanished with the sag of his shoulders.

"Wister is a friend," he said, and a smile was unveiled to test Parric's reaction. "He keeps us knowing about the places outside. He's going to tell us when he can come and see us and bring us out when it's all over. Out there. When it's over."

"Well, take my word for it," Parric said. "It's over. And Wister's coming. But you know that already, don't you? He's been in contact with you recently."

"He told us you were coming," Yasher said, a hand nervously rubbing at his pate. "Like he told us about the others. He said they wanted to take away the city and drive us into places that are dying with the Plague. He said we couldn't let him do that or we would all die. Terribly. We didn't want to do that."

Parric shook his head slowly. "Don't you people have comunits or something? Don't you talk with anyone but Wister?"

"Baron did . . . does when he has the time. He says it's true. It's hard for us now, but we're going to be alive when everything is over."

"And the people?"

The bald man pulled at the tatters of his clothes. "There was a one. A one with a dressing like yours. He wanted to talk with Baron, but Baron wouldn't do it because of what Wister had said. He said we had to get rid of them because they were bringing the illness inside."

188

"And you believed him."

Yasher appealed for and received a sympathetic murmur from his people. "How could we not? He knew how to work all the things here when they started slowing down. He knew how to get the food and the lights and the heat and the cool. He knew all those things. None of us did, so we had to believe as he said. And he was right. He said you could tell a man was dying when he wouldn't die. There was one in the people who was hit many times and he still wouldn't die." He looked to a man of similar age, a red-haired shadow who nodded his collaboration. "He wouldn't die, I tell you, and so we knew Baron was right."

"The man's name is Will," Parric said, "and he still isn't dead."

He turned, pointed to Dix, and a wailing began, was cut off when Yasher shouted for quiet, his face speckled now with perspiration. "Rogue," he whispered, and Parric felt the electric panic that blossomed from the men, the women, and transmitted itself to the whimpering children.

"Not a Rogue," he said sharply when the storm readied to break. "An android. A good one. A fine one not touched by the Plague." He grabbed at Yasher's arm and dragged him to Dix. "Touch him, damnit," he said, and the bald man swallowed, reached out and yelped when Dix snared his wrist, pushed his palm to his cheek and rubbed it there. When he let go, Yasher blinked stupidly.

"Listen," Parric said softly, so softly Yasher leaned forward in spite of himself, "he was there when you killed the others, and he is here now when you tried to kill me and her. Twice, old man, he hasn't been killed, but he and I can kill you all if . . ."

He stopped, shook his head and wondered why he was wasting his time threatening children with demons.

A boy, ribbed and filthy, broke from a woman and stood in front of the android. Dix looked down, and a man behind him moved as though to restrain him, thought better of it and buried himself in the crowd.

The boy, kicking at the floor, smiled shyly, puffed his chest and strutted back to the woman who raised a hand to strike him.

"Don't," Dix said.

The woman looked to Yasher, who hesitated before shaking his head. Then he turned to Parric. "These men who came here, this man here who came with them . . . Baron was . . . right . . . and we were told that they, he, came from a place—"

"I come from the same place," Parric said. "And if I am infected, then so are all of you. But I was born out there, old man, and I'm not dead yet."

Yasher lifted a finger to point at Dix, at the girl, at the people in the room. Then he folded the finger into a fist. "I don't understand."

Parric considered, came up with a way to tell the bald man that he and the others had been duped, conned, raised like experimental animals in a laboratory watched over and nurtured by two men who would rule. But it wasn't the time, and he knew he wouldn't be believed even if Courtney awakened just then and supported everything he said. He became impatient. He glared and felt a curious distaste at the way the people cringed. To them he was no less than a Rogue, a monster of nightmares who had accompanied their waking. The position was unpleasant.

He pointed to the girl. "Can you take care of her? Where is your Di?"

"Di?" Yasher frowned, again looking to the others for a definition and receiving nothing but stares.

"A Di, you Plaguesotted idiot!" Parric yelled. "A Diagmed. Don't you have diagunits around here? What do you do when you get sick? What happens when someone breaks a leg or an arm? Don't you have anyone who can help the girl?"

"The women are good with that," the bald man said quickly, and motioned several to his heaving side. "She's only bumped on the head, mister. She'll be all right."

Parric doubted and strode to the table. His hands moved rapidly over Courtney's hair, came away dry after locating the lump where she had been struck. He reached into his cloak, smiled at the backstep Yasher performed, and pulled out a capsule he forced into her mouth, pushing it back until she swallowed convulsively. "That will help her pain," he explained, more softly than he'd intended. "Now you, Yasher, will take me to Baron."

This time there was no hesitation, nor was there another attempt at reasserting control. The bald man rushed around the table and, after issuing several weak orders no one hurried to obey, led Parric out of the room into the hall and back to the staircase. Not discounting subterfuge, Parric checked behind them frequently to see that they weren't being followed.

"Why not the lifts?" he asked when Yasher stepped onto the landing. "What's the matter with them?"

"They're not working," the bald man muttered and began climbing two steps at a time before Parric could ask him another question.

Five more stories, and they were in another corridor, wider and darker than the one they'd just left. Here, however, the carpeting was still intact, the hallway furnishings still fastened to their royal blue walls. But a fine layer of dust kicked up by their boots made Parric frown.

He raised a hand, but Yasher had stopped in front of a door carved of wood and polished near to glass. The bald man wiped his palms nervously on his buttocks. He reached out, but Parric stopped him from opening it. He wanted no last signals to snatch away his prize, no final heroics to rob him of his right.

Yasher backed away when Parric took hold of the brass

knob in the door's center, one arm flung over his face just below his eyes.

"What is it?" Parric said. "A bomb or something?"

Yasher shook his head.

And so it comes, Parric thought. He touched the clasp lightly, then turned the knob and flung the door inward. Stepped over the threshold. Reached behind him to palm up the light.

There was a large blue chair to his left, flanked by footstools and stands for holding glasses. On the right, a rounded gaming table with a chess piece, a rook, alone in its center. The rest of the set lay scattered on the floor. Several chairs less imposing than the first, several paintings on the walls dulled without a cleaning. There was no window.

A bed jutted far into the room from the opposite wall. It was canopied in a red silken material that matched the sheet drawn up to the chin of Lemmy Baron. Parric blinked to adjust to the indirect lighting, then clamped a hand stiffly over his nose and mouth. A stride, and another, and he was at the bedside, looking down at the decomposing putrescence that had been his enemy.

He raised a fist to the ceiling and filled the room with an anguished moan that rose in pitch until his voice broke into a single word he screamed over and over and over again while he pounded the air, lifted a chair and shattered it against a wall, grabbed at the gaming table in a sobbing frenzy and flung it into the corridor, scattered the stools and stands and tore the paintings from their wires.

Dropped to his knees in the center of the room.

But the invocation, incantation, summoning wail of his father's name did nothing to bring life back to the thing in the bed.

*   *   *

He left the room, walking. Closed the door behind him, gently. Wiped the tears from his face and looked for Yasher who was sitting on the floor near the landing. Parric stood over him until the watery eyes looked up in an uncomprehending apology.

Parric felt old. And tired. Too tired to breathe.

"How?" he said, kicking lightly at the bald man's legs. "When?"

Yasher lowered his eyes and stared at his hands clasped over his stomach.

"You owe me," Parric said. "Tell me how."

"It was that fight," the bald man said, lifting one shoulder in anticipation of a blow, keeping it raised though none was struck. "He fought with us. He always did, so we knew he was thinking of us and taking care of us. It was near the end when the man who wanted to talk threw a knife and it stuck in his side. I picked him up and carried him back. All the way back. All by myself. The others didn't know. I told them Baron had fallen and hit his head." His palms pressed together, hard, and rubbed. "I brought him up here and put him into the bed. When Wister called, Baron made me answer and told me what to say. Wister said it wouldn't be long because no one else would come near the city now. They'd be warned that we weren't to be fooled with. He was right. We weren't."

Parric dropped to his haunches. Cupped a hand to his chin and rocked slowly, listening.

"Then he died. I was sitting in the blue chair telling him how the day went and he was dead. There was blood all over the bed, and he'd said nothing, nothing at all while I talked him to death.

"So then I got a couple of the others and told them what Wister had said and what happened to Baron. We decided not to say anything to the rest. They would run away and it would be all over. Wister wouldn't want us for his city if

193

he knew Baron wasn't around. So when he called after that, we said Baron wasn't around, that he was out someplace. On a trip to the Sectors. Anyplace at all. Once, when Wister got mad, we put one of the boys into a bed in another room, and lying down with the lights not right, he looked like Baron and Wister never thought about it."

"How many days?" Parric said.

Yasher frowned.

"How many days after the fight did he live?"

"I don't know. I think it was three, or four, or something like that."

"Three or four. No more. Are you sure it was no more than three or four days?"

Yasher thought, then nodded, looked surprised when Parric rose and offered him a hand. He hesitated, took it and heaved himself to his feet. He said, "Are you going to tell Wister?" and ran for the stairs at Parric's laughter, born deep in his throat as he shook his head, then he bent back to let his voice bellow through the halls. He staggered to one wall, bounced off with his shoulder and struck the other. He tripped over a chair, a table, a portion of his shadow. He leaned against the spiraled railing around the landing and looked down at the bald man's fleeing figure. He shouted meaningless words that were interrupted by his laughter, and his legs weakened, lost him, let him slide to the floor while he held the railing posts and rested his forehead against the smooth-cool metal.

Three or four days.

Dorin had lived for a week after the assault. He had outlived his enemy. He had killed him without knowing it.

Three or four days.

Not only had the dragons become toothless and their fire gone cold, but their leader was a sham, a spectre, a scarecrow rotting.

There was a stirring below. He crawled to the top step and looked down. Two people were arguing—one small, the other large. The smaller one shoved at the larger and ran past him, taking the stairs two at a time until, rounding the last curve below him she looked up. Parric brought his legs around in front of him and waited until Courtney had reached the landing and was seated with him. There was a stiff dirty cloth tied around her head. He touched it, and did nothing when she pushed his cloak back over his shoulders.

"You found him," she said.

"He's dead. And now you can say what you weren't supposed to when the tree almost caught us."

When she kept silent, he glanced at her, was caught by the softening of the blue he'd once thought was discolored ice. Even her hair seemed closer to the sun, though he knew it was only his imagination. But he had to reach out, to stroke it once and follow its fall to the curve of her back. Then he stopped, and crossed his hands over his chest: a sheet of uncontrollable tension was beginning to tear. He pressed hard, but the fissure widened, moving painfully from his abdomen to his lungs where the air came in darts through his barely parted lips. A pressure along his back, a hand at his neck. He choked, and the stairwell swayed toward him, receded and forced him to close his eyes to shut out the vertigo. A whispering in his ear, an urging, a medicine for the pain that swelled his breast until it exploded and he was held, crying and damning the streak in his hair.

When they returned to the room, Yasher was waiting with only the men. He stepped quickly away from the chair set in the middle of the floor as Parric approached, and seemed not to notice the small mocking bow sent to his back. Parric sat, and faced them.

"Don't worry about it," he said into the silence. "There's nothing wrong with me that a good meal wouldn't cure right now. Could you get me . . . us something to eat?'' He looked around the room. ''And where is Will? Yasher, if you're trying anything else—''

Courtney stilled him with a touch. ''He said the children shouldn't be in rags. While you were gone, he took a couple of the younger men and went off somewhere. He seemed to think he could break into some of the clothing stores.''

''He doesn't speak much,'' the bald man said.

''He says enough,'' Parric said, and jerked away from a poke at his shoulder. The android was beginning to bother him, more so than he would have thought a few days before. It was as though Dix was teasing him somehow, vanishing and reappearing like a vagrant wind; yet, Courtney accepted him virtually without question, as did the Baron's dupes. So what was it, then, that kept him from accepting what seemed to be inevitable? What the hell was the old man trying to prove?

''Food,'' Courtney reminded him. ''You can sit there and think all day, but I have to have something to eat soon.''

''Baron,'' Yasher said apologetically, ''had the keys.'' He pointed to an alcove off to the right. ''The place is empty now. We've been going to other buildings, looking.''

''What keys?'' Courtney said. ''I never saw any keys.''

''I think,'' Parric said, ''he means the codes for the central storage area. We have the same thing to a lesser degree back at Town. The ovenwalls, the freezes, they're not infinite suppliers in and of themselves, so each family would have a time to restock, with credivault approval when the city was functioning.''

Yasher nodded, losing his fear of Parric in the conversation and drawing a chair from the tangle along the walls. ''Baron knew,'' he said eagerly, ''and would get us what we needed when we needed it. None of us were here when the Plague—''

196

"And you never got the proper codes from your leader because he had to be needed."

Yasher did not care for the remark, but he was forced reluctantly into admitting its possibility. The other men, meanwhile, had pushed and shoved themselves into forming a half-circle on the bare floor, closing the gap between the two chairs. Parric looked at them quickly, not trying to memorize faces, but he was slowed by the animation he noticed rekindled in their expressions. He knew he was no telepath, but nevertheless he didn't like what they were thinking.

He cleared his throat, squirmed until Courtney knelt beside him and rested a light hand on his thigh. She knew, and he could have slapped the smug expression that masked her face. He glanced up at the ceiling, then, and prayed that Dix had found some clothes sooner than expected, would return to help lift this new and unbidden burden, as yet undefined, from his shoulders. He still had Wister to deal with, and he didn't want the emotions he apparently was stirring.

But Dix was gone, and not gone.

He jumped when the bald man coughed.

"Can you . . ." Yasher chewed thoughtfully on his thick lips. "Can you get us food? We can't do much anymore. We have to go too far, and the children, the women . . ." and he shrugged sadly.

"I think so," Courtney blurted before he could reply. "It'll take time, but I think we can help," and she poked at his shoulder until he nodded without thinking, was taken aback by the nearly palatable gratitude in the smiles he faced.

"We're not going to promise anything," he amended quickly. "I don't want you to get your hopes up."

"We'll help," Yasher said. "I don't know what we can do, but we'll help." He paused, then, and tried unsuccessfully to appear unconcerned. "And you . . ."

"Parric. My name is Parric."

"Parric. Are you . . . going to . . . going to still hate us?"

Had he a moment to think, he would have said he didn't honestly know, but the anticipation of his answer refused him the luxury of more than a few seconds' evaluation. "No," he said. "There's nothing here to hate."

"When will you start?" one of the men asked. "Can you start now?"

A chorus, then, of rapid-shot questions, suggestions, and several minor arguments for the ordering of priorities. It was all moving too rapidly for Parric to grasp without making himself dizzy, and he rose with a promise to do what he could and grabbed Courtney's hand to pull her from the room. Walking, then, until they were down in the lobby, staring at the banners until the darkness faded them; outside, then, and shaking his head at the contrast of a still light sky and the evening below.

"You shouldn't have said that," he told her finally as they walked without purpose, not noting their direction. "It's not what I wanted, and you know it."

"It's not what you wanted before," she said. "But that was before. Baron's dead."

"And I couldn't kill him."

"So you couldn't kill him." She stepped in front of him and pushed at his chest. "Is that all you ever did back in that big wonderful heaven of yours? Is that all you did, going around from town to town killing people?" She shook her head to answer her own question; and the smile that kept the cold from her eyes reminded him of Judith and the way she would mark the trail of his mind before he'd even found it himself. "You're lost, aren't you? You're really lost."

"All right, stop it. You're not telling me anything I don't know already."

198

"Well, that's fine, Mr. Orion Parric, but when in Plaguéd damnation are you going to decide what to do about it?"

He looked at her unbelievingly. What she said wasn't right, she was asking too much; and when he said so, almost barking his protest, she scoffed and poked him again.

"What's the matter, Orion? What do you need, time?"

"Of course, I need time, you idiot. Everything's happening so fast, I need time to think about it. I need time to see what's going on. Why can't you see that?"

"What I see," she said, "is a man no better or worse than anyone else. At least, in knowing what he wants. But you haven't got the time, Orion. There isn't the time you think you need."

He walked away from her and stood in the middle of an intersection. Dream One had been shattered, and now he was standing in the center of the wreckage of Dream Number Two: the city was blind at night, as blind as he had been, stumbling through the mountains.

And suddenly the city was small, far smaller than he had imagined.

Courtney followed him as he continued to wander, staying clear of the buildings, watching as the moon rose and the glimmering facades took on a faint luminescence.

Not blind, then, but adaptive. Lights for the sun, lights for the moon.

He heard her walking several paces behind him. He turned and waited for her to catch up, holding out his hands in a silencing gesture when she raised one of her own to continue her badgering.

"There's still Wister," he said. "Or have you forgotten our Redlin king?"

"I haven't," she said coldly. "Believe me, I haven't."

The fire returned. He grinned and settled the cloak on

his shoulders. "I'll make you a deal," he said, and laughed when she groaned her exasperation. "No, a real deal this time. I won't try to kid you."

"What are you going to do, try to kill him, too?"

The fire flared at the edge of her voice, and he walked away quickly, forcing her into a trot to keep up. "No, I may not have to," he said. "And I'll bet you're surprised."

"I am."

"Fine. Then this is my deal: I'll stick around here long enough to wait for Wister. While I'm here, I . . . Will and I will see what we can do to find those codes these people need. Once they have all that, they can get themselves back to normal and there won't be any more trouble."

"And if you do that, Wister will move right in and you'll be back where you started."

"Started?" He almost halted, but the driving was still too strong. "Started? I haven't started anything, girl, I haven't been anywhere to start from. You just remember what I said. Will and his damned pushing are bad enough. I don't need you, too."

"Pushing? I didn't see that he was pushing you, Orion."

"That's because you don't know him as well as I do."

XII

HE SLEPT ALONE in a room cleared just for him. The corpses had become the living, had set themselves to clearing the debris they'd scattered throughout the conapt building. He hadn't much liked what he'd seen and tried to discourage their open adoration with scowls and minor curses, but they hadn't been deterred and it wasn't long before he hid in the room and looked out the windows at the sky and the city. And what he saw were faces coalesced into one, and all his drained fury rekindled and cast thick black smoke over low warnings of sanity.

He waited for Dix. The old man didn't return.

He waited for Courtney; she didn't arrive. A faint twist of fear for their safety twice sent him to the door, and twice he halted in the act of opening. They wouldn't harm them now, he told himself; and the way Courtney was behaving, she probably wouldn't want his brand of rescue anyway. Apparently, she of all the others didn't care for knights on limping chargers.

In the morning, with Will still absent, he had Yasher show him the rooms that Baron used. They took up the entire floor on which his body was found, and Parric spent most of his time in one, a comunit center that Yasher pretended no knowledge of its workings. The storage block was here, and Parric took one quick look at the settings needed before throwing up his hands.

"Look," he said when Yasher backed away from his anger, "do you see these buttons here? Seven of them, right? All you—"

"We already tried," the bald man said. "We pressed each one slowly, in all the combinations. But we couldn't get any food. It's broken, isn't it?"

Parric shook his head. "No, it isn't. Now look again, and stop interrupting. You see, every conapt in this building, or rather, every family that used to live here had its own personal code. It had to, see, for the correct credivault billings. But with so many people and so many businesses that would have access to storage, the possibilities of duplication were too great. So I would guess—and I'm basing all this on the place where I come from—I would guess that each of the Sectors had its own primary coding. You had to know that, then use a private series before things would function. What we have to do, then, is find out what this Sector's code was, see. And since this is the Hive, I'd guess further that the Sector was subdivided, which means all we have to do is look in the immediate area instead of the whole Winded thing."

"Couldn't we just break into the wall? Maybe the numbers are there."

Parric scratched at his beard. "Yasher, every one of these ovenwalls, these in this building, are linked by a common coding of some sort. If we go smashing through and accidentally trigger something, we could Plague the entire system. So, we go elsewhere, where breaking anything won't affect us."

"But if those code things were private, would anyone mark them down? They would have to know those things."

"Right again, and so what we'll do is check on the businesses—offices, for example, where the workers could get lunches or snacks or something like that. With

202

personnel changeover, the primary would almost have to be displayed.''

''Then they'd steal them when they got home.''

Parric looked at the bald man and wondered how someone so old had survived so long without learning a thing about the place where he lived. ''It goes without saying,'' he told him, ''that Sector or Segment codes would be targeted. Not usable anywhere else.'' He took the man's arm and moved him toward the comunit wall. ''You know how to use this, right? You can use the vione as well as the comlink?''

Yasher nodded.

''Okay, then. I want you to stay here all the time. Activate the things. I'm going to start with the building next door and as soon as I find the first code, I'll call you and you try it.''

''And if it doesn't work?''

''We keep trying.''

''But we couldn't find the right numbers!''

''Yasher, you haven't been listening, and you haven't been thinking. I said the Sector and Segment codes would be locked. But that wouldn't have done Baron any good, because a child with time on his hands could easily stumble across the personals. It's obvious, since you said you've already worked the combinations, that Baron did some research and some unlocking. Instead of just combinations of seven . . .'' and he spread his hands, waiting patiently until Yasher finally nodded.

''He kept us,'' the bald man said sadly.

''He had to do it. Without that, he had no power.''

''So you will look for us?''

Parric grinned. ''You may have gotten used to living on crumbs, but I haven't. I've got to have my meals. And regularly.''

On his way down to the lobby, he met Courtney. She

was trying to get the children to play a Redlin game, but they were listless, their attention spans too short to pay heed to the simplest of rules. He watched for a moment, then called her aside.

"Are you going out for the kill already?" she said.

"I told you I don't need that," he said. "Look, I'm not sure about the power sources of this place. It's obvious the riots damaged a lot, and just as obvious there are things still working, though I doubt they will be for long—if I'd been the government in this place, I would have shut down the piles so nothing would happen in case of an emergency."

"Very good," she said, and didn't move when a fist was raised in her face.

"I told you to stop it, girl! What I'm saying is, there must be alternative energy sources somewhere, or these lights wouldn't be on where they are. I don't know—solar cells or something like that. Anyway, these people must have found a maintenance area in here. Those bulbs don't last forever. Get someone to show you where, then dig up what you can get and get this place looking bright again."

"Why? If you can't find food, we'll have to move."

"If the people aren't hanging around in all this gloom, girl, they might be able to think ahead for a change, and that will be to our advantage."

"And who is 'our'?"

He glared at her, turned on his heel and left the building, calling to three men who had been waiting for him on the stairs. They moved immediately into the adjacent building and covered it as rapidly as they could. By midafternoon, they'd found nothing in four, and he was beginning to resent the pouts the men were incapable of hiding. By the time they reached the corner, an office of something called Everlasting Assurance, two of the men had weakened from the climbing and were unable to walk. Parric and the last man left them sobbing helplessly on the street and broke through the plateglass front of the main floor. They ignored the small lobby and headed directly for the restrec areas they'd discovered covered a portion of each working level.

"Hey," the man said when they'd stumbled into the fourth such section. "What's this over here?"

Parric ran in, slowed when his chest ached and his side felt as though it would split. What he saw was an unusually plain ovenwall designed for quick and inexpensive meals. He grinned and slapped the man on the back.

"Now what?" the man said, grinning blackly.

"Now we do the worst things imaginable," and he found a chair with a loose leg, pried it off and attacked the 'wall at its chromium base. The man quickly joined him, and within minutes they'd exposed most of the workings, enough so that Parric was able to search for the enscribed digits he was seeking. And when his eyes began to sting and water from the close staring, he wished the owners of Everlasting Assurance had had the foresight to engrave the figures on the wall instead of using whatever method they had to enlighten their employees.

And when he found them, they were over a dozen. He groaned and punched weakly at his thighs.

"What?" the man asked.

"Look at all those damned numbers! I didn't know they'd be so big. It'll take us forever to learn them until we locate a working comunit for Yasher."

The man stared, then fetched the remains of the chair they had dismembered. He poked at the plastic back, then pointed at Parric's cloak. "You have the knife?"

In less than five minutes, they had carved the series into the back and had found a vione in an office several floors above them. Hurrying, Parric twice jumbled the coding for Yasher's link and was surprised to feel the man's calming hand patting his back. He looked up and grinned, then made the connection. Yasher and several others laughed when his face rippled across the screen, and he waved back at them before speaking.

"Yasher, listen to me. Below the seven buttons there are six others. Try what I have here and see what happens." And pray, he thought, that the supplies haven't run out, decayed, been stolen. He read off the first six digits, then sat back and waited while Yasher repeated them and one of the women did the coding. Disappointment was immediate, but Parric didn't give up until the entire series had been tried. "All right," he said quickly, "don't worry about a thing. This is only the first one, you know. Maybe it had a private segment all its own for some reason or other. We'll try again in another building. Don't go away."

He broke the link, stared at the chair back, then shrugged and led his partner to the street where he saw that the other two had not left, but were waiting patiently. He explained what had happened and what had to be done. They were too slow traveling as a quartet, so he split them into two teams. And though he was heartened by their eagerness to redeem themselves, he wondered how long their energy would last. Then he set up the parameters of their search and, with a further warning of the dangers of a jumbled power system, let them go.

By nightfall he was back, surly, and covered with the grime of a dozen deflating failures.

Courtney continued to avoid him; and when he did catch her eye, she only bowed mockingly and reached down to pat the top of her boots.

He sat alone in the main room and stared at the far wall, at the blank grey comunit screen and the series of activation devices which Yasher had kept polished. A small boy played silently on the floor in front of it, paying no attention to Parric. The bald man had told him earlier there were several men scattered along the outskirts of the Hive, keeping watch for the rats who filtered in from outlying

Sectors, looking for the Outfolk Baron said might some-day come to murder them all. Sometimes, Yasher had admitted, they called in just because it was lonely. And other times, they just stopped calling.

"A lousy way to live," Parric had said, and instantly regretted it because he knew it sounded as though he was dispensing pity where none had been solicited.

And now, observing the child's mute play, he realized it was the first time all day that he had been able to do any thinking at all. The hours of frustration had passed too quickly and were too full to be sucked into the bath of sympathy he wanted to wash over himself. But with the moments available, he still had too much to do. His stomach was noisy, and he glared at the comunit screen waiting for a solution to illuminate the room. Instead, he kept envisioning the encoding channels, the digits, and thinking that Yasher had told him they had patiently run through all the combinations, all of them, and nothing had happened. No one had mentioned the possibility of an exhausted supply, and had they done so, he would have doubted it loudly; with the size of the 'plex population so dramatically, terrifyingly reduced in so short a time, there had to be literally megatons of food just waiting some-where below them. The problem was how to tap it. And he bitterly congratulated himself for such a brilliant observation.

The boy, meanwhile, had taken up a collection of small pebbles and was tossing them against the wall, watching the place where they landed and covering it with tiny squares chipped from the floor. When the pebbles were done, he made some inaudible calculations, swept up the chips and began again. Parric, slouched in his chair, decided to test himself by figuring out the game, and thought he had a slight grip on its key when a pebble dropped onto an already marked space, and the boy pouted.

"What's the matter?" Parric said.

The boy stared at him in surprise. "You can't have two on the same place," he said as though it should have been obvious. "There's no room. You have to start again."

"Oh," Parric said. "Sorry you lost."

"It's only a game," the boy said.

Then don't take it so seriously, he thought with a silent laugh at the child's scowling return to the pebbles and chips. Two in one space. What in the name—and he straightened, grabbing fistfuls of hair until he yelped. The boy looked up again, unsure whether or not to run for the door. Parric smiled an apology. "Sorry," he said, "but I was just punishing myself."

"Why?"

"Because I'm stupid," he said. "Listen, will you do me a favor and go get Yasher for me? I have to tell him something."

The boy glanced doubtfully at the screen, and Parric assured him he would do the watching until he returned. Another second's pause, and the boy raced from the room, returning in less than a minute with the bald man.

"Listen," Parric said before Yasher had opened his mouth, "you tried all the combinations without getting anything, right? Or at least you tried to do them all, at any rate. Answer me this, then: did you ever double the numbers? I mean something like four-two-one-three-three-whatever? Did you ever do that?"

"Baron never said—"

Parric grinned and relaxed, folding his hands over his stomach and leaning his head back to stare at the ceiling. He asked for a torch and was told there was none; he asked if they had a means of starting a fire and they said they didn't know how. "All right, then, the lights in that building, the one where I first called you, they don't work for some reason. But that man and I cut the numbers we

208

told you into the back of a chair. It's dark, but send that guy over there to fetch it.''

''Why?''

''Why? Because I'm hungry, that's why.''

Yasher hesitated, and Parric rose, grabbed his shoulder and shoved him toward the door, repeating his order until the bald man nodded and ran. Parric waited. The word spread, and soon there was a small crowd in front of him, not pressing but staring, and among them but keeping to the rear was Courtney. He smiled at her and nodded. Reluctantly, she shouldered her way to him.

''You look silly with that grin on your face,'' she said. ''And your beard needs cutting.''

''You said that once before,'' he said. ''I'll cut it in the morning if it pleases you so much.''

''Please yourself,'' she said, and glared when he laughed.

And when finally Yasher and the man returned with the chair back, Parric snatched it from them and hurried to the nearest ovenwall. Courtney had managed to locate the maintenance pen and there was now sufficient light to give the entire floor a semblance of dayglow. It infected the women to giggles, the children to quiet laughter, and there was a subtly pitched expectancy almost electric in its effect.

''See,'' Parric said, pointing to the crude scratchings, ''this young man of yours—''

''He's called Daniel,'' a woman said proudly.

''Fine. Daniel. Well, when I read off the numbers to him, I told him to put down everything. And I remember muttering about the slashes you see here under the numbers. I didn't know if they meant anything. They do.''

And he took the first six digits and coded them, doubling each figure over a slash. ''I was wrong,'' he said as

209

he worked. "I was wrong when I said the Segment codes would be posted. They probably weren't, you see. They were probably locked into the system, and all the employee had to do was punch out some kind of shortened code peculiar to the office or wherever. So. Baron jumped the locking. You couldn't get the 'wall to work because you needed the Segment as well as the primary and personal."

"He held us," Yasher explained to the others.

"He did that," Parric said, and stepped back, wiping his hands against his shirt. "All right. Very slowly, I want you to start the combinations on the personals. Somebody keep track of them."

"What about the rest of the numbers?"

Parric looked for the questioner, and saw it was Courtney. "The first six will contain the Sector and Segment. We have no use for the others because they're undoubtedly strictly for that particular office."

"Are you sure?"

He blinked, then rubbed the side of his nose. "No," he said, "but why not try it?"

"You do it," Yasher said suddenly, and when Parric balked, he added, "Please. We want you to."

Parric wanted to protest. He wanted to explain that none of this would do them any good if he was right and the 'wall became operative. But he could see no immediate graceful or proper way to back out. He agreed. And twenty minutes later, the first silvered package slid steaming into its tray.

Hours. There was no counting.

They would live now, he thought as he paced the corridor outside the room. They would live and multiply and one of these days Wister would come by and take it all from them with those words of his. No matter how unfair things had been for himself, he felt an untapped source of simmering rage at the rainbow they'd been handed, and the clouds coming to take it away. He stood in front of a shattered wall mirror and saw his face fractured a dozen times, unrecognizable and unintentionally fierce. He tilted his head and the images shifted. Behind him, laughter, the high sounds of impromptu games and songs, the occasional muffling of voices as warm and solid foods were ingested. And they came to him, confidently and without fear, pressed trays into his hands, cups and utensils. He set them all at his feet, having eaten his fill from the first ovenwall offering, and tried not to laugh when he saw the adults as well as children sneaking out and snatching them back.

Will had returned in the middle of the party, burdened with bright cloth and gleaming footgear. Courtney had kissed him, the children blessed him, and sometime later, they'd been left alone, in front of the mirror.

Will had said nothing, plucking only at the sling that cradled his arm.

"Is it bad?" Parric asked finally.

"It'll fix."

Courtney poked her head out of the room, saw them and vanished. Parric had started after her, changed his mind without explanation.

"It wasn't your fault, was it?"

Dix kept silent.

"It's hard, Will. I remember the day you and Mathew left Central for wherever it was. I saw him . . . running, I think, and you going right with him just like you did with Dorin. I wished the Plague on you then, Will, you and Mathew and all those other smug and safe bastards who kept looking at me as if they expected miracles. There was one of those experimental Towns, like Grandfather had when he met you. I wanted to go inside and look around, to see what it had been like, but I didn't. I kept straight on the road as if it didn't exist. Straight on, Will, until I hit

211

Redlin, and Wister. I knew you were coming, you know. Mathew called me just before I left.''

A flurry of laughter made him turn, but the door remained closed.

"Why . . . why didn't you catch up to me at Redlin? You must have known what would happen to me there.''

"Here,'' the old man said, "was more important.''

"Dorin. He never let up, never stopped.''

Will stepped to his side. Parric saw the images doubled in the mirror. "Dorin,'' the old man said, "is dead, Orion. You and your brother now.''

"Will, am I going to die?''

"I told you once, Orion. I'm not a god.''

"These people, Will . . . Will, I still have to do what I came to do. Slightly different, but I have to do it. Will you be around?''

"If you need me.''

The old man had left, then. Parric stayed alone.

He stared at his images, and suddenly heard the quiet. Frowning, he went into the room and saw them all gaping at the comunit. A lower segment of the screen was lighted, nearly blinded with static, and Yasher was speaking softly into the lipgrille. When he had done and the screen was grey, he turned, stumbled over nothing when Parric raised an eyebrow in question. No one spoke. Parric knew. He pointed an order for them to stay, glanced at Will before running back to his room to pick up his cloak. Halfway down the stairwell, Courtney joined him, his own cloak pinned to her shift to keep its bulk from slipping and tripping her. He made no move to detain her, only took her arm and kept her at his side.

"We made a deal,'' he reminded her accusing glare. "I kept my word.''

"You haven't finished.''

"For a change, you're right,'' he said, and once on the outside began a slow steady running that took them down the center of the boulevard to the uppermost Walkway level. There was a moon, but its light was without warmth and created shadows within shadows, and enlarged the rubble Baron's people had not yet cleared. He tripped several times but never fell, only stumbled until his balance returned.

"Why are we running?" Courtney asked, her words as halting as her breathing.

"I want to meet him and get it over with."

"But he'll be there in the morning. Why don't we wait? He's not going to move at night, not when he knows less than us about the city."

"It will be in the morning," Parric said. "But where I want. My choice."

They arrived at the bridge's eastern end without incident. The buildings glowed in the twilight cast, but he could see nothing on the opposite side, neither movement nor lights nor even the sounds of cautious approach. He sat against the Walkway's rusted lip and wrapped his cloak tightly against the nightchill. Courtney sat with him, not touching, and while he thought she finally found some sleep, he only watched the moon fall, the sky shade from black to pale blue. Then he reached out and nudged her side until she lifted her head and blinked away her dreams. Her face momentarily lost the harshness she'd set against him; but when she remembered, and saw where they were, she refused his assistance and stood, slowly.

The wind was a constant. At his back, his face, threatening to tip him first to one side then the other. He scrubbed his hands over his face, brushed his fingers through his hair. His hands vanished into the folds of the cloak, reappeared with their daggers, vanished again and he was emptyhanded. Then he stepped out of the shadow of the building into the sunlight.

Waiting.

Courtney stood by the railing, holding it with both

hands, and he saw her looking down to the comettail water.

Thirty paces to bring him away from the Hive and into the open, and he saw figures stirring on the other side, advancing rapidly, at a run, dodging the rubble and apparently unaware they were being watched.

He waited.

Out of the glare of the windows on the opposite shore they resolved themselves: four Hunters, Wister, and Lynna. Parric tried to see behind them, searching for Shem and Lilly, but the group that came at him seemed to be all that there were.

And when one of the Hunters suddenly shouted and dropped to one knee, his weapon aimed, Parric spread his arms and opened his hands. Standing. In the wind.

Confusion, consternation, before Wister broke from the group and stopped ten meters from Parric. His hair was blown back from his face, red tunic and cloak a mockery of colors that laced the thin clouds rising with the sun. He didn't appear to be surprised. Or disappointed.

"You didn't kill me," he said, shouting over the wind. He patted his side. "My Di knows how to treat me, see."

"Did you bring him with you?"

Wister laughed and looked back over his shoulder. The Hunters were down in firing position, and Lynna was behind them, her hair bound in a tight silken cap.

"Baron is dead," Parric said.

"I thought as much, but I couldn't be sure. Why aren't you dead, too?"

"You have your secrets, I have mine."

Wister nodded his approval of the answer, then scowled. Parric, in spite of himself, turned around. There was a group of ragged, spindly men standing in a row at the bridge's edge. Several held clubs, the rest battered projectile weapons. Yasher and the one called Daniel stood in their center. They said nothing, made no sign they had seen Parric's angry look.

Dix stood off to one side.

Parric nodded. Turned back. Wister was now an arm's length away. They no longer had to shout.

"Your cityplex army, Mr. Wister," Parric said. "They got your call, in case you were wondering."

Wister fought to keep his cloak closed over his chest. Uncertainty, Parric thought with unaccustomed elation; the Plagueborn bastard's finally gotten himself afraid.

"This is my city," Wister said suddenly. "*My* city," and his voice rose to carry. "I've come to show you the way to Redlin. This isn't Philayork, you know. It's Redlin, now."

Parric shook his head, his lips profaning a smile. "It's an evil place, old man. You were right. It does something to you. It takes hold and you can't get out."

"But I told Baron—"

"Baron's dead."

"—that you were to be held until I got here." He stepped to his left and waved at Yasher. "You'll be rewarded for this, you know. Anyplace you want to live, you can. I promised Baron, and I promise you."

"You murdered Dorin."

"Nonsense! I wasn't even here."

"Here, there, you still murdered him. Right where you're standing now he might have died." And his laugh was cut short when the old man moved quickly back toward the center of the bridge. "And where is Shem, our old friend and teacher?"

"Redlin," Wister said. "He has to help me there, you know."

"Does he expect you back?"

"Of course!"

"Pity."

215

His left hand held a dagger, flipped it to his right, back to his left.

"They'll kill you," Wister whispered, taking a short pace away from Parric. He gestured to the Hunters, who had risen, their rifles still at the ready but less sure of their position. "They'll kill you before you can kill me."

"Then we'll all die," Parric said, "and maybe only the women will be left when it's over."

Wister stiffened, then jerked around until he faced Parric. His cheeks reddened and what words he had were strangled in the convulsions of his throat. Lynna pushed through the line of Hunters, and Parric saw the excitement in her face, the rise and fall of her breasts beneath the elaborate garment never meant for walking. He knew, and was repelled, that she was seeing Thomas again, his death and the deaths of too many others. Her smile when she noticed his stare was feral, her hands clasping and releasing the folds of her cloak.

Parric nodded to her, and grinned.

And when it happened, it happened without a word.

Lynna grabbed for a Hunter's rifle, struggled and wrenched it free. She lifted it awkwardly, trying to aim at Parric's chest. A weapon cracked behind him and her face looked stunned while the back of her head shattered and there was blood on the man behind her.

Wister screamed and lunged. Parric dropped the dagger and caught the Redliner by the tunic. They wrestled without advantage, grunting only as Parric sought to rid himself of the surprise at the old man's strength.

Lynna collapsed, face down, her hair running red.

A Hunter turned and vomited into the road.

Another dropped his rifle and ran.

Parric was thrown against the railing, pushed off and his

216

hands encircled Wister's throat while Wister clawed at his wrists.

Courtney stood silently, her cheeks damp.

Will stood unmoving.

A third Hunter fell with a chasm in his neck.

The fourth ducked behind a supporting post for the empty canopy and fired. A man tried and failed to scream as he fell. Projectiles snapped.

Wister sagged, reached up and clawed at Parric's eyes.

The Hunter killed another.

Wister struck the railing, was turned by his own momentum and draped over at the waist.

Two long steps and Parric had his legs. He lifted and held him. The old man snatched at the railing's supports. Parric released him. Wister clung with one hand, his eyes wide, his mouth open. Parric lifted a boot to smash the fingers, but the wind shoved him off balance.

The Hunter dropped his rifle, clutched at a bleeding shoulder and tried to stagger back over the bridge. He called out to his compatriot who had dropped crying to his knees after retching. They looked at each other.

Courtney knelt in front of Wister.

Parric moved.

She reached through the railing and raked her nails from forehead to chin.

The old man screamed.

All the way down.

Wind.

The comettail river.

Parric stood by while Yasher ordered his men to care for the wounded Hunter. Then they left when it became apparent Parric had nothing for them, not even his thanks.

There was still a sensation of knifing in his eye, and Courtney made him kneel on the road while she daubed at the blood with her sleeve, assuring him it was only a gash in the corner and he would not be blinded.

"We killed him," she said finally, and her trembling matched his own and they clung for a moment until they were calmed. A long sunbright moment cooled by the wind.

"Now what?" she asked.

"Town Central," he said. "I've done what I had to do. Now I can go home."

She shook her head slowly. "And what about Yasher and the others? Are you going to leave them here alone?"

"They can take care of themselves, girl."

"They'd do better if you showed them how. Baron's dead. Your father killed him."

He stared at the windows that multiplied the sun. It was happening again. He felt it worming a trail through the wreckage of his dreams. He thought of Town Central and the use it could put to the city he had. No. He didn't have a city. Yasher had it. Courtney had it. It wasn't his city.

He leaned on her shoulder, and she helped him to stand. He saw Dix move from his position at the end of the bridge, come toward him steadily, stop.

"Tell him," Courtney said to the old man.

"Won't listen," Dix said. "But I could go back. Have to get this arm done anyway. Tell them what's here."

Parric wondered if he could find a way to establish a comlink with Central.

"If he wanted, he could get those people fed, on their feet again. Take time, of course. But he could get it working again."

He considered the power to be tapped, the resources he had now made available to the slowly growing ContiGov web. Ignoring Courtney's fussing at his throat, he watched as Dix scratched his jaw thoughtfully.

"I could be back in half a year, a little more maybe. Bring some techs, people like that."

A lightness at his shoulders.

"Won't be easy."

He looked down, and she was folding Dorin's cloak into a small, tight bundle she handed to Dix. She had ripped off the clasp and as he watched, she threw it into the river.

"It's too big," he said, looking at the Hive.

"I thought you were a gambler," she said.

"That was my brother."

They stared at him, then, and he clenched a fist to smash the look, opened his hand to stroke the side of his beard. "Do you two know the chances of pulling off something like this?" he said, trying to shatter their unnerving quiet. "I can imagine how many Redlins there are out there just waiting for the right time to come in and set themselves up like Baron and Wister. It'll kill us, you know that, don't you?"

"If I get started," Dix said, holding his bundle close to his side, "I could be back with spring."

The Hive.

People learning, relearning, stumbling, he thought, because Will isn't the only one who wasn't a god.

"One condition," he said suddenly.

"Mathew—"

"I know, I know, but damnit, I'm not Mathew and I'm not Dorin. One condition, Will. You've got to promise me."

"All right."

"Will, you're going to have to come back and teach me."

Dix took his hand, placed Dorin's cloak in it. Then he bowed to Courtney and started across the bridge. Parric wouldn't turn. He watched instead the blinding windows and decided that the men of *Alpha* should have at least one familiar place to come home to.

"Orion?"

He looked down to Courtney who was watching behind him.

"Can he bring back other . . . you know, androids?"

"He'd better," Parric said. "I don't want to turn on all the lights in this place only to have it turn into another Redlin."

He waited, then, for the depression, the weight of his family, and when it didn't come, when he felt only an anxious urge to get off the bridge and prod things into motion, he shivered.

"You're cold," she said.

"I ought to know if I'm cold or not, girl, and I'm not."

"Courtney," she said. "My name is Courtney."

"Damn," he said. "I guess I learn slow."